Chills skipped up her spine, but she forced herself to stand straight and greet this next hurdle straight on. Deep breath in…slow exhalation. But even that failed to calm her racing heart or lessen the knocking of her knees.

As for offering a serene smile—she wasn't about to attempt one. Only a fool would smile at the shark swimming toward them.

Henry's voice drifted to her, so clear she knew he was standing in the corridor outside the waiting room door. "Miss Tate is in her father's office. If you'll come this way, sir?"

"That will be all," replied a deep, masculine voice that ground Delanie's thoughts to a screeching, nerve-grating halt.

No! Her mind must be pl

But there was no mista
accent that she hadn't he
in her dreams. That she'd

"Sir," Henry sputtered. "I

"Leave us!" The clipped order blew open the lid on painful memories she'd tucked away long ago.

The man from her past was here. Was *he* the corporate raider? The man with the wherewithal and the ruthless bent to strip everything from her?

Her gaze swept the room to find a way out, her pulse racing so fast she was lightheaded. Were the walls closing in on her?

No, jus

For as long as **Janette Kenny** can remember, plots and characters have taken up residence in her head. Her parents, both voracious readers, read her the classics when she was a child. That gave birth to a deep love for literature, and allowed her to travel to exotic locales—those found between the covers of books. Janette's artist mother encouraged her yen to write. As an adolescent she began creating cartoons featuring her dad as the hero, with plots that focused on the misadventures on their family farm, and she stuffed them in the nightly newspaper for him to find. To her frustration, her sketches paled in comparison with her captions.

Though she dabbled with articles, she didn't fully embrace her dream to write novels until years later, when she was a busy cosmetologist making a name for herself in her own salon. That was when she decided to write the type of stories she'd been reading—romances.

Once the writing bug bit, an incurable passion consumed her to create stories and people them. Still, it was seven more years and that many novels before she saw her first historical romance published. Now that she's also writing contemporary romances for Mills & Boon she finally knows that a full-time career in writing is closer to reality.

Janette shares her home and free time with a chow-shepherd mix pup she rescued from the pound, who aspires to be a lap dog. She invites you to visit her website at www.jankenny.com. She loves to hear from readers—e-mail her at janette@jankenny.com

Recent titles by the same author:

ILLEGITIMATE TYCOON *(Bad Blood)*
CAPTURED AND CROWNED
INNOCENT IN THE ITALIAN'S PASSION
PROUD REVENGE, PASSIONATE WEDLOCK

INNOCENT OF
HIS CLAIM

BY
JANETTE KENNY

MILLS &
BOON

First published in Great Britain 2012
by Mills & Boon, an imprint of Harlequin (UK) Limited.
Harlequin (UK) Limited, Eton House, 18-24 Paradise Road,
Richmond, Surrey TW9 1SR

© Janette Kenny 2012

ISBN: 978 0 263 89133 1

Harlequin (UK) policy is to use papers that are natural, renewable and recyclable products and made from wood grown in sustainable forests. The logging and manufacturing process conform to the legal environmental regulations of the country of origin.

Printed and bound in Spain
by Blackprint CPI, Barcelona

INNOCENT OF HIS CLAIM

CHAPTER ONE

"It's done." Henry returned the telephone to its austere black cradle with a decisive click, his face as stoic as the marble busts in David Tate's executive office in central London. "The takeover of Tate Unlimited is complete."

Delanie sat perfectly still and stared across the desk at her father's massive, empty chair. Most women thrust into her situation would be a puddle of tears. Fretful. Scared. But she felt curiously numb. Detached, as if she was watching someone else go through the death of a parent, the subsequent ordeal of a swift hostile takeover of his corporation and now a very uncertain future.

Though she'd been unable to display grief at his funeral, she had at least shown respect. Considering her relationship with her father, even that was a lot.

"My bid to exclude the house and my family's personal assets?" she asked, holding onto the hope that she had salvaged something from her father's empire.

Henry, who'd been her father's attorney for as long as she could remember and who she'd affectionately called Uncle Henry all of her life, shook his head, his papery lips pulled into a thin line that sent her hopes plummeting. "All gone. However the new owner has trumped your bid to buy Elite Affair with a counter offer."

"What does he want?" she asked.

Not that it mattered. Her only means to negotiate a deal in

the first place hinged on selling the vintage cars. But those were gone, leaving her with nothing tangible to trade or sell.

"His solicitor wouldn't say, stating the owner will inform us of the details upon his arrival," Henry said.

Of course, more waiting. More drama added to this corporate piracy.

She huffed out a weary breath and pushed to her feet, smoothing her dress over her hips. Fittingly, she was garbed in a somber black Dolce and Gabbana sheath, although it made her pale complexion seem waxy and lifeless. Right now she felt bloodless but was too angry to surrender.

The fall of her father's company had been inevitable, yet she'd hoped that the corporate dragon breathing fire down on them for the past two weeks would have the decency to show respect. That he would at least listen to her request. That the unknown entity hiding behind the group called Varsi Dynamics was, in fact, human and not a machine or monster.

Now she wasn't sure. She wasn't sure of anything.

It would be so easy to toss in the proverbial towel. Certainly people would understand that losing both parents and every worldly thing she possessed in such a short span of time was simply too much for her to bear. But her pride wouldn't let her give in to pity and pride was all she had left.

Narrow shoulders squared, she strode to the draped window and gathered her courage around her for this meeting with the tycoon who had gobbled up everything her father had owned. Everything she owned and valued as well, damn him!

She flung back the drapes and stared at the cold rain streaking down the mullioned windows. Steel-gray clouds barred the sun from making an appearance.

The gloomy weather was appropriate to laying her father and his wretched empire to rest once and for all. If she could just get back what was hers....

"Do we at least now know who's behind Varsi Dynamics?" she asked as she faced her father's loyal attorney.

"No." Henry consulted his Baume & Mercier watch, a gift for service long ago. The brown leather band now seemed too bulky and masculine for his bony wrist that was only slightly bigger than her own. "But we shall soon find out. He's scheduled to arrive at quarter past two."

Any time then, she thought. "Good. I want to get this over with and go home."

Only she didn't have a home anymore. She had nothing. So where would she go? Impose on friends? Pound the streets looking for a job?

Delanie tried to tuck an errant strand of hair behind her ear but the tremor that continued to rock through her undermined the effort. She gave it up with a heavy sigh and let the pale gold strand fall as it had repeatedly done at the cemetery.

If she were prone to outbursts then this would be the ideal time to have one. What kind of man would demand that this meeting be held in the closed offices of Tate Unlimited on the heels of her father's burial?

Perhaps a visceral man with horns and a tail. Clearly he was a man without principles.

The man behind Varsi Dynamics had launched his takeover on Tate Unlimited in her father's last hours. Before her father was interred at the Tate family plot at Sumpton Park, the corporate shark had gained control of her father's assets, right down to the furniture in the mansion and the fleet of Rolls Royces in the garages.

"I imagine the new owner will take great delight in personally firing everyone on staff," she groused as she stopped behind the burgundy leather chair her father had ruled from.

Henry fidgeted with his crimson-and-gold striped tie, the first sign that he wasn't quite as calm as he let on. "Actually, his solicitor assured me that all Tate employees would remain on staff through a six-month vetting period."

She blinked, that news the one ray of sun on this gloomy day. "That's a surprise."

"Indeed," Henry said, consulting his watch again. "Time to go below stairs to meet and show him up. Wouldn't want the gent wandering around the building and getting lost. Will you be all right alone?"

His concern brought a bittersweet smile to her face. "Yes, I'll be fine."

Henry gave a crisp nod and left, his gait swift and sure for a man his age.

Silence thrummed in the room that held only bitter memories. No, she wouldn't miss Tate Unlimited. But Elite Affair, the company her father had swindled out of her, meant everything to her. It was her dream. Her means to support herself. Her freedom from a man's control.

She was anything but fine, she thought as her palms pressed into the sumptuous leather back of the executive chair.

The scent of spice wafted in the air. Her father's aftershave. Faint, as if he'd just stepped out of the office.

The old urge to run pinged through her like a cold pounding rain and she shivered. To her father, a woman's main purpose was to marry well and produce an heir. A male heir, according to the verbal barbs he'd flung at her mother for failing to uphold her duty.

In his eyes, Delanie was no better. Her fingers dug into the leather as his biting diatribes played over and over in her mind. A failure. A liability. No better than her mother.

If he hadn't blackmailed her to stay on this past year she would have left. In hindsight she should have done that, for she'd ended up with nothing anyway—unless by some miracle she could meet the new owner's counteroffer.

The *ding* of the elevator echoed dully down the corridor. Masculine footsteps pounded the marble floor like an advancing army. Her pulse rose with each step.

The waiting was over.

He was here.

Chills skipped up her spine, but she forced herself to stand straight and greet this next hurdle straight on. Deep breath in, slow exhalation. But even that failed to calm her racing heart or lessen the knocking of her knees.

As for offering a serene smile, she wasn't about to attempt one. Only a fool would smile at the shark swimming toward them.

Henry's voice drifted to her, so clear she knew he was standing in the corridor outside the waiting-room door. "Miss Tate is in her father's office. If you'll come this way, sir."

"That will be all," replied a deep masculine voice that ground Delanie's thoughts to a screeching, nerve-grating halt.

No! Her mind must be playing cruel tricks on her.

But there was no mistaking that husk of an Italian accent that she hadn't heard in ten long years except in her dreams. That she'd wished never to hear again.

"Sir," Henry sputtered. "I insist I be on hand…"

"Leave us!" The clipped order blew open the lid on painful memories she'd tucked away long ago.

The man from her past was here. But why? Was he the corporate raider, the one with the wherewithal and ruthless bent to strip everything from her?

Her gaze swept the room to find a way out; her pulse raced so fast she was light-headed. Were the walls closing in on her?

No, just her past.

The waiting-room door slammed shut, likely in Henry's face. She jumped in heels that suddenly pinched, her skin pebbling and her heart thundering with each determined step that brought Marco closer.

Footsteps stopped outside the office door. She swallowed hard. Had Marco paused to straighten his tie—a quirk he'd done often because he detested wearing one? Or, on a wilder thought that mirrored her rising hysteria, was he sharpening his teeth for the proverbial kill?

Her heart thundered, her body swayed as the dizzying rush of memories swirled around her like a choking fog. Each sec-

ond nipped along her skin, chipping away at the confidence
she tried desperately to shore up.

The man she'd thought never to see again stepped into the
office and shut the door behind him with a deafening click.
Her traitorous eyes drank him in: tall and commanding, broad
shoulders racked tight. Breathtakingly handsome.

Piercing dark eyes set in a classic face drilled into her, im-
paling her to the spot. "*Ciao,* Delanie."

Her fingernails dug into her father's chair, likely scoring
the leather. But it remained her only shield against the enemy.

Enemy... In her wildest imaginings, she had never
guessed that the mystery owner of Varsi Dynamic was Marco
Vincienta, her ex-fiancé. The man who'd held her heart in his
powerful hands and crushed it without remorse.

There could only be one reason for him to take over Tate
Unlimited and demand that she meet him here a scant hour
after her father's funeral. Revenge.

She swallowed, her throat parched, the spacious room
shrinking as the powerful throb of his aura reached out to
encircle her. Trap her.

"Marco," she said, her voice catching over his name that
she'd once said lovingly, the emotionally wounded man that
she'd foolishly thought she could heal with her love.

He looked larger, stronger, colder. His lean torso was in
top physical form, more so than memory served. His wealth
of dark hair that she'd loved running her fingers through was
clipped short in a fashionable style, yet an errant curl strayed
onto his broad tanned forehead to hint at his rebel soul.

He was far more handsome and intense than she remembered. Far more dangerous-looking. Hungry. Like a caged
wolf she'd seen at the zoo, its cool gaze scanning the crowd,
searching for easy prey.

Only Marco stared straight at her. The look of a predator
who'd tracked down his quarry. Who had it cornered and was
moments away from pouncing.

Perspiration beaded her forehead and dampened the deep V between her breasts. It took supreme effort to stand straight and keep her head high, refusing to show fear or any weakness.

"So you are the man behind Varsi Dynamics," she said.

A rapacious smile curved his chiseled lips that had once played so tenderly over her eager flesh, awakening sensations she'd never felt before or since he'd exited her life. Sensations that maddeningly still caused heat to curl in her belly.

She hated that odd loss of self-control, that awareness of him on that level. Hated him as much as she'd once loved him. Perhaps more now that she knew he'd been the one to put her through such hell the past few weeks.

"It is one of my lesser acquisitions."

"Lesser?" She couldn't hide her surprise.

The wolf's smile widened. "Hard to believe that the young bastard you and your father stole a company from amassed a fortune and the power to take down a titan."

"I had nothing to do with what my father did," she said, earning a snort from him. "Everything I felt for you was real."

"Yes, just like your tearful confession of family abuse, revealed after I confronted you and your father with the truth, after I said I was done with you." His dark eyes were void of emotion. "It was too little too late. Perhaps if you'd told me your story before you betrayed me…"

"I never betrayed you," she spat. "Why are you so blind to the truth? Why must you think the worst…"

He sliced the air between them with a hand and she stammered to a halt. "History. What happened then has nothing to do with why I'm here now."

She forced her chin up and met his cold gaze head-on. "That's rather difficult to believe after you've systematically stripped me of everything."

The tailored sleeves of his jacket pulled into perfect pleats as he crossed his arms over his chest, his face an impassive mask. He was a stranger, worlds away from the young Italian she'd lost her heart to. An older, harder version of the dynamic lover who'd broken her heart.

"I'm in need of your services," he said sharply.

She blinked, stunned speechless. As a wedding planner? Lover? Did it matter when either was cruel to ask of her?

"Is this a joke?"

"Not at all," he said. "I want you to come to Italy with me today."

For a moment she couldn't think, couldn't get past those same words he'd spoken long ago. Come to Italy with me... Leave the hell of her life. Leave her mother at her father's mercy...

She couldn't do it then. She wouldn't now.

"No way," she said. "The only reason I honored your order to be here today was to hear your counteroffer to my bid for Elite Affair."

One dark brow winged up. "This is my counteroffer. Come to Italy and plan a wedding. If you please the bride and me then Elite Affair will be yours."

Could it be that simple? No, there would be nothing simple about being around Marco, seeing him fawn over his bride.

It would be emotional hell for her. Torture. But, she thought, her mind catching on the carrot he dangled before her, in the end she would gain Elite Affair—if she could trust him to uphold his end of the bargain.

Her eyes met his intense ones and her foolish heart fluttered. It was a dangerous game. But right now she had absolutely nothing to lose and everything to gain.

"All right. But I can plan your wedding from London and send one of my consultants to ensure the events go off perfectly."

He shook his head. "No. You will be there from start to finish or the deal is off."

She shoved her father's massive chair aside and rounded

the desk, facing him. "Why? What does it matter as long as your bride is happy?"

He drove his fingers through his hair, then pinned her with a look so intense she had to lean against the desk to keep from swaying. "Because the bride insists that you be there to oversee every detail."

"And you would do anything for your bride," she said.

"*Sí*. I want her day to be perfect."

Exactly what every groom should want, except this man had once asked her to marry him. The man who had vowed to stand by her. Believe her. Protect her.

Marco had failed miserably at all three. What was to stop him from stringing her along to get his way?

"Not good enough," she said. "I demand a guarantee in writing that I'll get my company back when the work is done."

"No. You get the company if your work is satisfactory to the bride."

"And if she nitpicks?"

"You have a reputation for pleasing the most finicky client."

"Within reason," she clarified.

He almost smiled. "You'll be amply compensated for your time."

And make a fool of herself over him again? She shook her head, having been down that rocky road before, having trusted him before. Never again.

"Forget it. I'll never agree to that."

"Don't make vows you can't keep," he said.

"Trust me, I can keep this one!"

He glared at her, a stone pillar of a man who had once been turgid hot flesh and blazing passion in her arms. Ancient history.

They had been a bright nova. They'd come together in a cataclysmic crash of passion only to fade into cold darkness when it ended. He'd hurt her more than she'd thought possible. Was still hurting her, she thought sourly.

"I never knew you, Marco, but then that's how you wanted it," she said, letting him see the pain and anguish that must be evident in her eyes. "You put up walls and shared very little about your past or your fears, and the dreams you wove for our future were hazy."

"Yet you were willing to marry me."

She bit her lip, wanting to deny it. But she couldn't. "I was young. Naive. I trusted you." Loved him.

Marco's brow snapped into a V as he jerked his gaze from her and mouthed a curse. Then he presented a broad rigid back to her, fists clenched at his sides.

She hadn't expected a like confession from him. That wouldn't be Marco. So why were tears stinging her eyes?

Dammit, she'd held her poise and dignity throughout the funeral. She certainly wouldn't give Marco the satisfaction of knowing how much he'd crushed her again. How close she was to crumbling into a heap.

Head high, she marched toward the door. There was no reason to stay, no use to try and negotiate with him. That would be up to Henry now.

No home. No job. Nothing but her pride.

"I am not finished with you," he said.

"Tough," she said, relieved her voice didn't betray her heartache, that her knees didn't buckle. "I'm finished with you."

A few more feet and she was closing the door behind her with that same resounding click she'd heard as he'd entered. A sob caught in her throat but she managed to choke it back as she ran across the waiting room toward an uncertain future.

CHAPTER TWO

Marco wrenched the door open with nearly enough force to pull the heavy oak panel off the bronze hinges. Amazing that just a few minutes in Delanie Tate's infuriating company could fling him right back into that chaotic mix of emotions he'd tried to run from all his life.

His disposition was soured by the fact his body stirred at being near her again. That his heart thundered despite the anger cracking like sheet lightning along his nerves.

No woman but Delanie had ever brought those explosive emotions out in him, but with that intense desire came fear. A cold choking fear that he'd never understood until he'd returned to Italy ten years ago and yanked the dark shroud off his past.

He should let Delanie go. Cut his losses now and go home. But as his eyes locked on her trim backside running across the waiting room, he knew he couldn't let her go. Not now. Not when he'd promised his sister that he would return to Italy with Delanie Tate.

He wouldn't gain her compliance by crossing swords with her. But he damned sure wasn't going to beg for her help either.

A smile flicked over his lips. He held what she wanted most. She would be the one begging.

"How much does Elite Affair mean to you?" he asked, just as she was a step away from sailing out the door.

She stopped, one hand pressed to the open doorjamb while the toe of one impossibly high black heel remained poised to push her out the door. Even in unrelieved black mourning, she was sexy as hell. And those damned shoes...

The strong, perfectly curved length of her leg and dainty foot in those take-me-now shoes brought back memories of her wearing similar footwear and nothing else. His body stirred, his blood heating to a most uncomfortable level. If not for the steely snap to her slender shoulders and the cool, almost hostile gaze she flung at him just then he would think the pose was staged to entice him.

"Well?" he prodded when she simply glared at him.

"You're enjoying your victory at my expense."

"Don't flatter yourself," he said. "My goal was to take down your father's empire."

"Which you did. Don't expect me to congratulate you."

He crossed his arms over his chest and leaned against the doorjamb, enjoying this side of her. When he'd met her she'd been a combination of playful and meek, leaning more to meek in her father's shadow.

But in the ensuing years Delanie had acquired bite and verve. The way she held herself and her ability to closet her emotions intrigued him. Not that he wanted to be intrigued again by this woman.

She'd tricked him once. He would never be so foolish as to totally trust her again.

Remembering that betrayal zinged an old burning sensation across his heart. "Are you going to answer my question?"

"Elite Affair means a great deal to me and you know it," she said, slender shoulders straight and back painfully stiff.

"Then use your head. If you walk out that door now you will toss away any chance of regaining total control of the business you built."

She went pale, or perhaps it was a trick of the light. "After what you've done, how can you expect me to trust you?"

"I don't," he said. "This is strictly business. I've taken the initiative to draft a mutually beneficial contract. Are you willing to listen to terms or do I fire your employees and liquidate Elite Affair?"

"You'd do that to a profitable business?"

"In a heartbeat."

Her small hands bunched at her sides and the mouth he'd dreamed of kissing into submission in the dead of night drew into a tight unyielding knot that slammed straight into his gut.

Dammit, he'd expected a tearful confession that she *had* worked with her father against him, followed by his magnanimous offer to hire her for his sister's wedding, with Delanie's reward being a fat check plus title to her company. But she was resisting him at every turn. Showing spunk and a stubborn bent that challenged him—aroused him.

Not that he would back off no matter what she said or did. He'd come this far and there was no retreat. No concession.

His gaze locked with hers and he caught that flicker of doubt. It was a battle of wills and in that he had the upper hand because he held what she wanted most. Elite Affair.

"Fine. We talk," she snapped, not sparing him a glance.

She had conceded as he'd expected her to do. So why didn't he feel victorious?

Delanie slammed the door she'd been about to escape through and strode back into her father's oppressive office, passing him with a swish of her long hair. Ever the reigning princess.

He loosed a smile, enjoying the sight of her full bottom beneath her unbecoming black dress. His gaze remained on those long dainty legs that were deceptively strong, that had once clung tightly to his hips in the throes of passion.

Certainly if he put his mind to it he could have her back in his arms, back in his bed. And that was a complication he had no intention of taking on. Too much was at stake to risk satisfying his libido no matter how tempting. And she damned sure was tempting!

Ironic that the only passion between them now was anger and that shimmered off her in sizzling waves. Even that set his pulse racing, he admitted, sobering instantly.

If only he could cease wanting her more than he'd ever wanted a woman. If only he could purge her from his system once and for all.

He gave his French cuffs a tug and followed her into the room, shutting the door and his emotions firmly behind him. She visibly jumped and he swore.

"Relax," he said. "I don't intend to pounce on you."

"Excuse me for not trusting you," she said, still presenting her painfully straight back to him.

He fisted his hands, resisting the urge to cross to her and force her to face him. Touching her would be a major mistake.

"That goes both ways, Delanie."

She whirled to face him, features pinched tight. "If you distrust me so, then why do you want to negotiate with me?"

"I don't," he said frankly. "As I told you before, you are the bride's choice."

"And you'd do anything to please her."

"Yes," he bit out, "but—"

"Including corporate rape," she interjected, chin thrust out and accusing eyes fixed on him.

He stiffened, the explanation poised on his tongue forgotten. "My takeover of Tate Unlimited was aboveboard."

"Perhaps," she said, chin up. "But your motive was revenge, proving you're no better than my father."

His fingers wadded into fists. "Never compare me to him."

The warning was given in the strong, flat monotone that always convinced his opponents to switch topics. Color instantly bloomed on her too-pale cheeks, like vibrant English roses blooming amid snow, but her chin remained up and her gaze glittered defiance.

"Are you denying you acted out of vengeance?" she asked.

"No. But if I was in the same league as your father I would overextend Tate Unlimited until it was destroyed, as he did to my vineyard."

Lines creased her delicate brow. "What?"

He drove his fingers through his hair and swallowed a curse. "Do not pretend you weren't aware of its downfall."

"I had no idea." She shook her head, voice soft, big blue eyes wide. "Please tell me the truth."

The look, the plea… That's all it took to shift his plans off kilter. To get him thinking about her. In his arms. In his bed.

Her innocent act was worthy of an award, he thought grimly.

"You were vice-president of Tate Unlimited. How could you not know when you had access to all corporate records?" he asked.

Color flooded her face and she looked away. "It was a token position. I served as his hostess at business functions and, as he termed it, a charming diversion to his potential clients during intense initial meetings."

He wouldn't allow himself to believe her, no matter how much he might want to. "Fine. Play innocent. It doesn't matter."

Her fists landed on the plush back of the chair. "I am not *playing* innocent. I am ignorant of what my father did to your family's company once he gained control, or why he would destroy something he obviously wanted so badly."

Her wide eyes pleaded with his, open, unguarded. He huffed out a breath. Swore.

"Sagrantino grapes are prized throughout Italy and the world and my family's winery grew the best. It was our legacy but few had heard of us outside of Italy because we couldn't produce enough to satisfy world demand." A muscle pulsed along his lean jaw. "That's why I sought your father out. I needed financial backing as well as a noted exporter who could place our wine worldwide. Once he had wrested control of my family's company, he destroyed it with gross mismanagement."

"I'm so sorry he did that to you."

"As am I, because his impatience and ignorance destroyed the vineyard."

It was time to let the past drop into the black hole of his memories and hammer the lid back on it. He was in control of all that David Tate had owned. That evened the score as far as he was concerned.

As for Delanie, she was back in his life only because of his vow to please his sister. Once she finished planning the wedding, it would be better for both of them if they never saw each other again.

"Your small company has achieved a degree of favorable notoriety," he said.

She gave him a long appraising look. "I'm surprised you noticed."

"It was brought to my attention."

His gaze drilled into hers as she stood behind her father's chair. "I'm giving you the chance to gain sole ownership of Elite Affair, debt-free, by successfully planning a lavish carte blanche wedding that will be photographed and reported worldwide."

She went absolutely still, eyes widening like saucers. "Why are you willing to hire me with our history between us?"

It was a sound question, especially considering what he'd done—storming the citadel and winning. "You are my sister's choice because of your company's promise to work with the bride to make her wedding special. Every plan you do is unique."

She crossed her arms beneath her bosom and gave the most unladylike snort, as if his compliment meant nothing to her and that almost made him smile. "Does your bride know that you are entrusting arrangements for her wedding to your former lover?"

He shook his head and let a rusty chuckle escape. This bolder side of Delanie was a welcome switch from the demure girl he'd known.

"I am not that trusting," he admitted. "The bride is my sister, Bella, and she wants someone who will understand her needs and abide by her wishes. She needs your special touch, Delanie."

Her eyes widened again and the faintest flush stole over her cheekbones. "I wasn't aware you had a sister."

"I didn't know myself until eight years ago." His hand cut the air, dismissing the topic from further inquiry. "It is complicated."

"I've discovered that many families are 'complicated' in ways that have some impact on an upcoming wedding," she said. "That's one reason we are selective in our clientele."

"Is that the only reason why you turned Bella down when she attempted to hire you two weeks ago?" he asked.

Her too-pale lips parted. "You can't be thinking that I knew she was your sister, because I swear that isn't the case. And even if I had known, my assistant handles all the initial calls. The moment he discovered the wedding was to take place in Italy, he would have politely declined and wished her well."

Which, according to Bella, is exactly what had happened. "So what will it be? Your agreement to plan Bella's wedding for title to your company or do we part company now?"

She bit her lip and frowned, then huffed out a breath and nodded as if coming to grips with her decision. "I'll do it. I'll have Henry send a contract to your solicitor by the weekend and we can go from there."

"That's too late. The wedding is two weeks from now."

"That's not nearly enough time," she sputtered. "Two months is not sufficient to orchestrate such a lavish affair."

"If we wait two months it will be clear why the bride is marrying so quickly. Understand?"

Her cheeks flushed a charming pink but she gave a jerky nod. "Yes. Well. That doesn't leave us much time."

"No," he said. "I had my attorney draft a contract for your review. Once you sign we can be off."

She stiffened up again. "We?"

"I'm in a time crunch and must return to Italy tonight. You'll come with me and oversee the details there."

"I can't," she said in a strained voice he'd never heard before, that touched something kindred in him. "My business and assistants are here."

"There is nothing that can't be done via the internet or phone," he said. "You'll have the best of both at your disposal."

She cupped her palms to her face, her slender shoulders trembling once. Twice.

That tremor had him fisting his hands to keep from reaching out to her, enfolding her slender form against his length. And that would be a mistake for then she would know how much she'd affected him.

Dammit, he wasn't going to let her get to him.

"Your answer, Delanie," he said. "Do you come with me? Or is the deal off?"

She pressed her lips together, throat working. "After all that has happened between us, do you honestly expect me to trust you and drop everything?"

"Yes, because I am entrusting you to organize the most important day in my sister's life."

She looked away, stilled, then she bobbed her head and he hoped to hell that meant she understood, that she would cease fighting him.

"I prefer my own contract," she said.

"As do I."

Her chin came up again and her gaze clashed with his. Only the tremor in her lower lip belied her total control.

"My contract is designed for my purposes but you are entitled to make minor changes to it if you like," she said.

He most certainly would do that. Ever since the disaster of dealing with David Tate, Marco had learned to manage his own affairs to the letter.

But this concession was doable. Perhaps even wise, for he would know what she expected and would be able to mount a countermove if necessary.

This time he held control and he would have Delanie close at hand again. And why the hell was he entertaining any thought of being close to her again?

His gaze raked over her, his brow furrowing. The black dress she wore encased the petite figure he remembered with aching clarity. She appeared gaunt and fragile. A deception, he was certain.

Marco paced to the heavily draped window and swore, painfully aware of what was at the heart of it. She'd intrigued him from the start. She still did.

But that didn't matter now. It was all in the past, and it would stay there. He had control over that part of him now.

Having her in Italy would prove that. By the time his sister was a happily married woman, Marco would have no doubt in his mind that walking away from Delanie had been the right choice ten years ago. He could finally purge her from his system.

"Fine. Give me your contract and I'll read it on the plane," he said, the decision easy as it suited both their purposes. "Now let's leave."

Delanie bit her lower lip again. No was the easy answer.

But he was holding out her dream on a silver salver. He also held her employees', really her only friends, future in his hands. She couldn't refuse.

And if she was honest with herself, a part of her didn't want to walk away. She could easily blame that lonely part of her heart that still held Marco Vincenta close, the part of her that wondered why he'd found her so lacking. That deep-in-the-night dream that his desertion had all been a horrid mistake and that they truly were meant for each other.

She was a fool for entertaining such fanciful thoughts, even for a moment, but she'd always been a fool for love where Marco was concerned. At least by taking this job she would be opening doors for herself in the future. That was her dream. That was what she would focus on instead of the tall handsome Italian whose touch made her bones melt.

"Okay," she said. "It won't take me more than an hour to pack."

He broke eye contact the moment her agreement was out, snapping a strong wrist up to consult a watch that looked masculine and expensive. "We leave now. I will buy you whatever you need once we get to Italy."

And that was the end of that argument, concluded before she could get her anger up. She made a quick stop at her minuscule office to collect the passport she'd needed for her dealings with Henry, her laptop, a contract and the jeans, jersey and comfortable sandals she'd left at work in case she decided to begin cleaning out her father's office today.

With the lot of it crammed into a small carryall along with the few toiletries she kept on hand there, she let Marco escort her from the building, barely having the time to thank Henry before she was ushered into a gleaming black sedan.

She pressed a hand to her stomach, the drive through London a blur while Marco sprawled beside her and talked on his mobile, speaking a language she barely recognized as Italian. Not that it would have mattered if she spoke it fluently. Each time the car zoomed around a corner, the steely length of his leg brushed hers and her mind simply shut off as another emotion exploded in her, one that had lain dormant for ten years.

But even if they hadn't touched, his presence simply commanded every inch of space. Commanded every second of her attention, leaving her all too aware of him as a powerful man.

Ruthless. Driven. She could see the end effect of what she'd glimpsed in him years ago.

Knowing she was powerless in his company played along her nerves until a discordant hum vibrated through her to leave her stomach knotted. Even shallow breaths pulled his essence deep into her lungs, bringing a flood of memories that made her throat clog with emotion best left untouched. In these close confines she was doubly aware of his control, his power, his sensuality.

Shifting away from him the best she could only brought his intense brown eyes slewing back to her. Her cheeks instantly turned red—she knew they must be because she felt the fire burning her skin.

"Is something wrong?" he asked when she had inched as far from him as possible.

Wrong? He had the gall to ask that when his large muscled form dominated the interior of the auto? When he'd taken everything from her?

She lifted her chin, aware diplomacy was necessary to avoid further conflict. "I was just giving you space."

His gaze narrowed, his lips pulling into an uncompromising line. "Are you? Because to me it looks as if you're avoiding my touch, even if that touch was no more than my arm or leg brushing against you. Accidentally brushed you, I would add."

What could she say to that and maintain this fragile peace? The truth. They'd had a wretched history of avoiding the truth when honesty mattered most. But then when she had been honest with him, he had still walked away from her. He had been the one to turn his back on her.

"Use your head. Less than an hour ago you stormed into my life and took everything from me in the wake of my father's burial," she said with a telling quaver in her voice that had her clenching her fingers in frustration, a habit she'd developed as a child when her father was venting his anger on her mother.

She'd been so good at hiding her emotions from her volatile father. But she'd failed miserably at that with Marco.

He knew when she was angry, hurt, cautious. But he never could guess the reason for her trouble and she'd been too ashamed to tell him everything.

Her cheeks burned at the old memory. In that regard he'd been right to accuse her of lying to him. To be angry. If only he had believed her when she finally revealed her shame…

"I'm physically and emotionally spent, Marco. You've won. I've agreed to come to Italy and plan your sister's wedding. But that's all you'll get from me," she added. "Is that clear?"

"Extremely! I want nothing more from you than what was agreed upon," he said, shoulders snapped into a rigid line.

"Good. I don't want any misconceptions," she said.

"There was never a doubt of your role or of mine," he said as the sedan thankfully came to a stop at the airport, ending the torture of him jostling against her time and again. "Ten years ago you were looking for a rich man with status, a man who would measure up to your and your father's precise standards. I was not that man then nor am I now."

She gaped, flabbergasted. "You can't believe that!"

"It is the truth."

He couldn't be more wrong, but to admit that would prompt questions she wasn't about to address. Her trust had been broken not once but twice by this man. She wasn't about to put it out there again.

Not that it mattered. He'd already slammed out of the car, leaving her alone and trembling. She pressed a hand to her middle and slumped against the seat.

A private jet—she'd never been able to tell one from the other—sat on the tarmac to her left, its stairs lowered to admit passengers. It didn't dawn on her that this was Marco's plane until she saw a crewman carrying her small duffel onto it.

Her door was wrenched opened a heartbeat later and cool brown eyes flecked with gold stared down at her. "Let's go."

She gave a nod and tried to extract herself from the car without his help. He mouthed a curse and assisted her to her feet, his large hand enveloping hers before she could protest, his skin warm against hers, his touch gentle and strong. Heat sped up her arm yet she shivered, liking his touch far too much and hating herself because of it.

The moment she gained her footing he dropped his hand from her and motioned her toward the plane. The message was clear: he didn't wish to touch her any more than she wished to be touched.

A lie, if her libido had a say, which it most certainly did not. She crossed the tarmac quickly and hoped once inside she could find a seat far removed from him.

Not a problem, she realized as she mounted the stairs and stepped into the private lair of an Italian wine baron. The interior was dressed in a classic, yet understated, design resplendent in rich browns, ivory and gold.

The flight attendant motioned Delanie to take a seat. She bit her lower lip—so many to choose from. Twin flight chairs. A large curved sofa that was far too intimate. Farther back more chairs and a table, likely utilized for meetings. Beyond that an open door that showed a glimpse of a bed.

Wishing to stay as far away from a bedroom as possible, she claimed one of the deep gold chairs up front with a smile to the attendant and a quick glance at her traveling companion. He passed her without sparing her a glance, the thick carpet muffling his steps yet cluing her in that he preferred the rear of the plane.

Fine by her, she thought irritably as the strategically positioned cushions conformed to her tired back and tense shoulders. He could shut himself up in his bedroom for all she cared. The lack of his presence after such a trying hour would be a welcome pleasure.

"We'll take off immediately so please fasten your seatbelt," the attendant told her before disappearing into a cabin up front.

Delanie obeyed without complaint and tried to relax, not an easy feat as she'd never been a seasoned traveler. In the Tate household, the only member who took holidays was her father.

Perhaps this wouldn't be so bad. The interior was quiet and comfortable and the chair was an absolute dream. If she managed to control her stress levels as the plane reached cruising altitude and leveled off then maybe she could nod off en route.

God knew she was tired enough to fall asleep standing up. The past week of dealing with doctors and attorneys and worried shareholders had drained her of her last reserves.

But total rest was still denied her.

Perhaps she could have dozed off if Marco's voice hadn't drifted to her. If her body hadn't come awake at the deep timbre that left her shaking.

He spoke in clipped Italian delivered so fast and fluently that with her meager knowledge she couldn't begin to translate. Was he really so much like her father, always engaged in some deal? Or was he delivering the news to Italy that he'd succeeded, that he'd brought Tate Unlimited to its knees?

That he had the millionaire's heiress in tow with the contract that she'd agreed to do his bidding safely in hand?

All of the above, she thought as a small degree of hysteria rippled through her. Could she have dreamt up a more intense working relationship? No!

Marco was the billionaire who had trumped her tyrannical father's millionaire status. He was the antithesis of power. He was her boss for the next two weeks.

He was the only man she'd fallen in love with. The only man she had ever loved physically and emotionally.

A hysterical laugh stuck in her throat as the plane sped through the clouds, carrying her into the unknown with a man who was more stranger to her than ever before. A man she'd hoped to cling to in the dead of night, who would be there for her until the day she drew her last breath. The man she'd spun dreams on.

Her only lover. Her hero.

Unwanted tears stung her eyes and she blinked them back. How very wrong she'd been.

Hopefully, once they arrived in Italy he would take himself off so she could breathe again. So she could think. So she could do her job and then escape back to London with sole ownership of her business in hand.

Only then could she focus on her career. On her future. On living in peace. That's all she wanted.

All she had to do to have that was endure two weeks in the company of the man who still left her weak-kneed. Who tormented her dreams in the dead of night.

She could do it. She had to. Failure wasn't an option.

CHAPTER THREE

Two hours into the flight, Marco ended the conference call and rubbed his gritty eyes. Sleep had been sporadic all week, a fact that could be blamed on the alluring beauty seated primly in the front of his plane.

His gaze zeroed in on her with unerring accuracy. She hadn't moved much since boarding the plane. Had she dozed off? Was she simply enjoying the flight, content knowing that she would get exactly what she'd wanted all along?

He shifted and damned his restlessness. It shouldn't matter to him if Delanie Tate was pleased or not. He'd never set out to spite her and he damned sure hadn't attempted to placate her.

In fact, before his sister's interference, he'd hoped to avoid her entirely during this shift in power. Delanie was a page from his past and he intended to keep her there.

Page? A wry smile tugged at his lips. No, she was a chapter at least. Perhaps even a book of pure trouble.

Still he hadn't wished to reread that episode anytime soon. But Bella's stubborn insistence on having Delanie as her wedding planner forced him to chose between pleasing himself or his sister.

He snorted. That had been no contest.

His sister's happiness came first.

That had put Delanie right back into his life.

While he'd been prepared to deal with her on a business level, he hadn't anticipated he would still find her unbelievably attractive. He'd never anticipated his body would react so at her nearness.

It was frustrating. Annoying. Unacceptable.

Dammit, he was a man in charge of his emotions. In control of his sex drive.

So why the hell was he shifting restlessly on the leather chair?

He swiped a hand down his face. This unwanted reaction to her was unacceptable on far too many levels.

If he had taken Delanie at her word, which he did not, he would have ordered the plane back to London and have her escorted off. He would have gladly let her plan his sister's wedding from there, thus freeing himself of her alluring company.

But he couldn't trust her. She'd betrayed him before when she'd sworn she loved him. There was nothing between them now but animosity on her part, and wariness on his own.

Since Elite Affair had turned down his sister once and then him a second time when he had upped the offer of money, he was left with one choice—force Delanie's hand. His takedown of Tate Unlimited was the perfect opportunity.

There was no other recourse, he reasoned, refusing to take pleasure from watching the dim light play over her hair. She worked for him now. More so than other contractors he was in league with, she needed to be watched and made accountable.

The only way he could achieve that was by maintaining total control of the situation. That was best done by having her under his thumb.

Easy enough to accomplish. Or it should have been.

Being physically close to Delanie was a totally different matter that he still didn't feel comfortable dealing with. But he would.

She aroused him on a deeper level than he liked and no amount of avoidance would change that. Even distancing himself from her on the plane hadn't worked because she'd been on his mind the entire time.

He swore and scanned the contract she'd pressed on him earlier. Since it was straightforward and clear, he signed it without ceremony and left his chair.

"Your contract is precise yet fair," he said, breaking the silence as he came to a stop behind her.

She started in her chair and looked back at him. The dark of her eyes nearly swallowed the clear blue.

"Thank you," she said. "I see no reason to make a straight-forward business arrangement complex."

Her voice held that breathy quality that lapped around his control like warm waves, threatening to erode his defenses. It was so tempting to relax and be taken out to that sea of passion they'd frolicked in long ago. Too tempting.

"I'm of a like mind," he said, planting his feet firmly in the here and now as he dropped onto the seat across from her.

The most charming flush stole across her cheekbones and he paused. Except for the unnatural stiffness in her narrow shoulders and the tilt of her head, she looked very much as she had when they'd met.

The years should have hardened her. Should have shown on her face. But all he saw was a reluctant surrender and a proud bearing that he admired.

"Tell me about her," Delanie said, her gaze fixed on his again.

He looked away so she wouldn't see he was softening to her again, that his control over remaining impassive was slipping through his fingers like warm grains of sand.

"My sister?" he asked, then smiled when she nodded. "Bella is beautiful and willful and far too seductive for her own good."

"Yet you love her."

He sobered at that assessment. Love. He had loved his grandparents. Had loved his mother and tried to love his cold father—a wasted effort. He'd been consumed with Delanie but had he loved her?

No, it couldn't have been love. Infatuation. Lust. When the truth came out he'd had no difficulty walking away from her.

So why did she cross his mind in the dead of night? Why did he catch himself comparing every woman he met with her?

His chest heaved as the answer skirted his mind—an answer that he always ignored, just as he always ignored that old gnawing sense of emptiness when it threatened to yawn away in his soul. Or the skitter that streaked up his spine.

Like now.

"Bella is my responsibility," he said. "I care for her."

"That's cold."

"That's reality. Bella resents me."

She blinked, her clear eyes fixed on his as if she could read his soul. "Why?"

He shifted on the seat, uncomfortable delving into this. Yet what was the use in holding his silence? She would find out soon enough from someone in the village or at the villa. He might as well be the first to break the news.

"Bella thought she was Antonio Cabriotini's only bastard," he said simply.

"Antonio Cabriotini?" she parroted.

"Our biological father," he said, glancing her way to gauge her reaction.

She shook her head and frowned. "I thought your parents were married."

Such naiveté. "The man who raised me, who gave me his name, was married to my mother but I wasn't his son. When he found out, he withdrew the closeness I'd always had with him."

For a moment Delanie couldn't breathe. Couldn't wrap her brain around what he was telling her. And then finally she got it with a breathless wham to her midsection.

She finally understood the reason behind those broad tense shoulders attempting a careless shrug, the motion as abrupt as a salute. His illegitimacy was the reason for the pain she caught lurking behind those dark fathomless eyes, pain at having the father he'd loved ripped from him. That was the change in him she couldn't quite put her finger on.

"How long have you known this?" she asked.

"Eight years."

The words were shot out without feeling, his gaze boring into hers now. Hard. Cold. Defiant.

But she heard the underlying pain in his voice as well. Caught the tiny tick of hurt that snapped like a sail along his taut bronzed cheek.

Her heart gave an odd thud and her hand shifted, a blink away from reaching out to him. She caught herself with a trembling clasp of her own hands.

How wrongly would he take it if she offered compassion? Considering their past, she doubted he would take it well. Yet hadn't they moved beyond the past pain? Weren't they old enough and wise enough to understand nothing untoward was meant by it? Now wasn't the time to dissect it to find out.

"I see," she said, nerves stretched so tight they hummed.

"Do you?" he asked. "Because I don't understand how my mama who claimed to have loved my papa could be unfaithful to him. I do not understand why nobody saw fit to tell me the truth until after my parents' deaths."

Hearing the anger in his voice, that telling drawl when he told her this, made her insides cramp in an oh-too-familiar pang of understanding. No wonder he had no faith in love. He would never open himself to an emotion he believed caused only pain. And wasn't she just as guilty of holding back from him? He was right. That was in the past. There was nothing she could say when Marco had never believed her anyway.

"You would likely be surprised by how many families hold dark secrets," she said, cheeks burning and stomach knotting at the troubled memories of her own childhood.

He snorted. "Nothing surprises me anymore."

How sad that he had become more jaded. But then, so

had she. Wasn't she afraid to trust? To surrender her heart and soul?

She shifted on the chair while her mind shoved away from that train of thought. "I gather your sister knew of her paternity before you did."

"By a month or so." He drove his fingers through his hair, sending the thick waves in disarray.

She caught a breath as an old memory ribboned through her of doing the same to his wealth of dark hair. Of holding him close to her on a sun-kissed beach, laughing with him, kissing him in a slow, deep burn until the world blurred to only them.

Ten years ago she'd been a hopeless dreamer, desperately wanting a hero. Her innocence had convinced her that when she looked deeply into his warm brown eyes she believed her world was complete with him in it.

She shook off those idyllic yesterdays like a cool rain on chilled skin and chanced a glance at him, hoping he wasn't looking at her in some sort of horror. But he stared off, brow furrowed, clearly troubled by something else.

"Did you know her?" she asked, grasping the thread of their conversation by its tail.

"No. We were strangers coming from vastly different backgrounds which complicated matters more. Since the start Bella has resented that I was named her guardian until she reached twenty-five," he said, clearly not of the same mind.

Delanie felt a commiserating pang with his sister, knowing how badly she'd ached to break free of her domineering father, hating that she'd waited and waited for her own dawn of independence. "How old is she now?"

"Twenty," he said, sliding her a knowing look.

The same age she had been when she'd met Marco. Willful. Emotional. And tangled in a wretched triangle with her parents, dreaming of freedom yet unwilling to put her frail mother at risk to grab what she wanted.

"Tell me more about Bella," she blurted out.

He shrugged, this time the movement less tense. "As I said she's young. Spoilt. Resentful."

"Of you?" Delanie guessed.

He laughed, but she caught the pained treble, the hint of worry that had her wanting to leave her seat and go to him. Hug him, comfort him. Sanity prevailed and she didn't, but it wasn't easy knowing his elite world wasn't perfect. And hadn't she hoped that would be the case? She was suddenly glad for the subdued light on board that hid the heat scorching her cheeks.

"Bella resents me, resents the world," he said, dark eyes on her again. "She needs a strong hand."

Of course he would think that! But hearing him admit he was controlling his sister proved her fears long ago were right. Or did they? Was she still using that as an excuse to hold back from giving her all again? From trusting?

She stared at the floor, admitting she'd lost herself in his arms that first time. Basking in the afterglow of love was new. Terrifying.

Still she'd loved Marco. She'd hoped that she was simply mistaken. But the second time they made love was more consuming, more earthshattering to her heart. Her soul.

My dear, I love your father, and he loves me in his own way, her mother had told her as she recuperated from a volatile night spent suffering her father's anger.

Delanie never forgot that night. Never forgot that love could hurt. That love could strip a woman of her independence. Perhaps even her sanity.

No love was worth that, Delanie had decided.

That realization had kept her from committing fully to Marco again. And wasn't she right in thinking that in time he would have slipped further into the role of dominator, perhaps even going to the depths her father had sunk to? That she would relive the hell her mother had had throughout their marriage?

Single was safer. Single was being free. So why was her body craving his possession again? Why was she so weak around Marco Vincienta?

"I seriously doubt your sister needs a man dominating her," she said and was instantly pinned in place with his fierce scowl.

Her heart raced but she hiked her chin up, determined not to tremble over the past that still bound her, refusing to cringe at Marco's command as she'd seen her mother do with her father countless times. Or worse, whimper when he physically abused her.

"You are an expert on these matters because?"

Delanie didn't understand why on earth she had thought that the intervening years might have finally made him believe her. Still, he'd asked so she would answer.

"My father was quick to rule with an iron hand or fist depending on his whim." He'd used it liberally on her mother to gain Delanie's compliance.

A ripe curse exploded from him. "I told you never to compare me to David Tate!"

"Then stop acting like him."

He frowned, brows drawn in a deep forbidding V over the classic slope of his nose. Time hung suspended between them, her heart supplying each tick of the seconds that raced past.

His fingers bunched into fists at his sides and her stomach flipped over. Ease up a bit. Marco won't hurt you. At least not that way. She knew it in her heart, her soul.

"Are you saying Tate hit you?" he asked, his dark gaze probing hers.

For an instant she almost thought he cared that she might have suffered physical abuse, though for her the emotional barbs scared her just as much. But she'd heard her father apologize for his deplorable behavior for too many years, and watched him break his promises.

"No, he never hit me," she said. "As I already told you, Father reserved his punishment for my mother."

"A lot can change in ten years."

That was an understatement considering she'd found herself trapped in an untenable situation. Since he hadn't believed her then, why show concern now?

She huffed out a breath, his curiosity annoying. Insulting even. It no longer mattered to her what he thought. She certainly didn't owe him an explanation.

His gaze narrowed, hardened. "Answer me."

Again with the demands. But avoiding the issue was more troubling that it was worth. Nothing could be gained by ignoring him.

"A lot can remain exactly the same as well," she said. "But to satisfy your curiosity, I stayed to ensure that my mother wasn't abused. It was the only promise that my father never broke to me."

Marco clenched his teeth against her bare-faced lie. He knew she was lying. Had known ten years ago. But if she was so insistent on pursuing her lies, then he would see how far she would go with them.

"What kept you there after her death?"

"You still don't get it, do you? My father did to me what he did to you. He gained control of my business and the only way I could get it back was to abide by his agreement. I was two months away from getting my company back from him when you launched your takeover."

She glared at the rich, powerful man who held all the cards and tried to forget there had been a time when she'd loved him with each breath she took. When she'd wanted to believe his every word. Wanted to trust him fully. A time when she wrestled between fear and desire.

"Now I'm doing your bidding to gain title to what is mine," she said.

His gaze remained remote. "You'll be amply compensated."

"I'll hold you to the letter of the contract," she said.

He smiled, the gesture brief and calculating. "As will I, Miss Tate. Which is why we will stop at the villa first so you can meet Bella and complete your survey."

Without another word he rose and walked to the rear of the plan, the soft snick of a door the only indication this inquisition was over. That he'd finally left her alone.

She crumbled in the chair and rubbed her forehead, emotionally spent. Despite his resentment of her, or perhaps because of it, he'd given her a golden opportunity to reclaim Elite Affair.

He was following her contract so far, so she couldn't very well complain on that quarter either. Still she wasn't about to let down her guard around him.

This was business. Nothing more. For that reason alone she had to keep her guard up. Had to see this event through to the end. Had to watch that he didn't double-cross her—that once the job was completed, Elite Affair reverted solely to her one hundred percent.

Only then would she be able to start over. To make a life for herself. To be independent for once in her life.

All she had to do was get through the next two weeks.

Moments after the plane smoothly landed at the San Francesco d'Assisi airport on the less hilly outskirts of Perugia, Marco escorted Delanie to a waiting sedan and they were off. He rarely used a driver unless he was entertaining a fellow businessman, preferring to handle the wheel himself down the *autostrada* as well as on the roads that bypassed walled towns and sliced through the patchwork of medieval fields of produce.

But the combination of too little sleep and the emotional upheaval of being near Delanie again curtailed that urge. He tapped a fist on his thigh, still vexed by the latter.

He should not find her attractive. He sure as hell shouldn't begin to believe her lies about her troubled childhood, not when he'd learned the truth. If David Tate had been the beast Delanie swore him to be, her mother would have broken free when she'd had the chance.

He needed his thoughts on the present. His relationship with Delanie was just business, pure and simple. That fact alone called for space between them. Though once they were in the backseat of the car she took that to the extreme and scrunched against the door as if waiting for the chance to jump free.

"I repeat, I am not going to pounce on you," he said.

Her gaze swung to him, a bit wild and overly wide. "I know it's just… You're so intense. So angry still."

He scowled, disliking that he was letting his emotions reign. She was so nervous he literally felt every quick breath she sucked in until his own equilibrium was spinning.

"My apologies then," he said. "It has been a very long day without sleep."

"For both of us." She heaved a sigh and directed her attention beyond the auto again. "It's beautiful here."

"*Il cuore verde d'Italia.* The green heart of Italy." He loved it. Respected it. Nurtured the land to the best of his ability and it rewarded him with kingly yields.

"You've always lived here?"

"For some time now," he said, not inclined to share more of the details of his life with her.

There was no point in it.

She faced him, her perfectly shaped head lifted, pale brows pulled over the proud tilt of her nose. "Your vineyards. Are they near here?"

"The vineyards I inherited or the land your father destroyed?" he asked when he knew damned good and well that the latter was what she meant.

Two swaths of red streaked across her cheekbones. "It always comes back to that, doesn't it?"

"It is not something one forgets."

"Or forgives," she said, frowning. "I'm so sorry Father did that—"

"Save it," he snapped. "I'm in no mood to hear your apology or excuses."

She shut her mouth, hurt he had jumped to conclusions when what she'd been about to say was "to us." Yes, it was horrific that her father had spitefully ruined the business that had been in Marco's family for generations. That he'd added another emotional scar to the ones Marco already suffered.

But the greatest tragedy of all was that Marco saw her as the enemy too, that he had refused to believe her then, that he couldn't find it in him to trust her now.

You don't trust him anymore either.

How funny he'd accused her of lying, of betraying him, when he too had broken his promise. He'd shattered her trust in him.

She heaved a sigh, sick at heart that nothing had changed. They were still two wounded souls, hurting each other because that was easier.

"I'm curious about the vineyard my father destroyed," she said, making herself clear.

He stared straight ahead, annoyed she was continuing her questions, vexed that the ripple of pain reflected in her clear blue eyes got to him, made him believe her innocence if only for a moment.

All an act. It had to be. And if he was wrong? If she was truly ignorant of her father's schemes? If she'd been blackmailed to comply with Tate's dictates?

What did it matter now? Too much had happened between them. He was more jaded than ever before and she was as well or she wouldn't be this cautious, this remote.

"Fine," she huffed out, crossing her arms and staring militantly out the window. "Forget I asked."

He caught himself smiling at her show of temper, admiring

that steel that ran down her spine. A gentleman would comply
with her request. But he was no gentleman.

"It is roughly twenty kilometers south of the villa. Half an
hour by car." He stared at her profile, willing her to face him.
"Less if I'm driving."

She continued her vigil out the window but he thought
some of the tension eased from her narrow shoulders, that the
slightest hint of a smile teased her soft lips. "How long before
we reach the villa?"

"It should not take more than twenty minutes," he said,
answering as calmly as she'd asked, keeping his tone low,
intimate, as she'd done.

It didn't require a response and she didn't offer one. That
was for the best. More than ever he needed to get back to the
reason she was here.

Theirs was simply a working relationship. Anything beyond that was too great a risk.

Yet instead of relaxing, his heart accelerated even more
during the drive to the Cabriotini villa. The easy explanation
was his own unease at returning here, far easier than admitting his thoughts were on Delanie.

The simple truth was this mansion wasn't home to him and
never would be. The moment he was away from it, he put the
man who'd lived and wasted his life and fortune here completely out of his thoughts.

If he could just do the same regarding the enticing woman
beside him. She'd plagued his sleep too often over the years.
He'd convinced himself he'd hated her.

A damned lie.

He distrusted her but he didn't hate her. He wanted her with
the same fire that had burned in him ten years ago.

The conundrum for him was how to put that fire out?

His gaze flicked to hers and his body stirred more than
it had in ages. What the hell was it about this woman? Dare

he hope he could get her out of his system? That he could move on?

Overindulgence. Too much of a good thing could sour a man. Perhaps that was what was needed now.

CHAPTER FOUR

DELANIE had caught glimpses of elegant mansions nestled among the hills throughout the drive and had expected Cabriotini Villa to be along the same order. But the moment the auto pulled into an iron-gated drive that swung open automatically, she knew this estate was far grander than any she'd seen so far. Perhaps more so than any she'd visited in England.

For one thing, the villa claimed a commanding view of the valley, perched on a knoll overlooking perfectly aligned fields of grapevines laden with plump purple and blush fruits. On the surrounding fields, groves of olives lined up in precise rows, their leaves shimmering silver in the sun, their black and deep green fruit glistening like jewels.

"Welcome to Cabriotini," Marco said as the driver sped up a long drive flanked by poplars standing like sentinels.

The sun popping through their dense tops created a dappled effect, as if they were waving Marco home. Only instead of a smile he wore a pensive expression as if he dreaded coming here.

"You don't care for your ancestral home, do you?" she asked at last.

"I am only here temporarily—this isn't my home. It's the estate bequeathed to me and Bella by the man who sired us, and it's where we've lived since discovering our paternity."

She blinked, stunned by his vehement tone. "That's a rather impersonal way to refer to your father and your sister."

He cut her a look that made her shiver. "Antonio Cabriotini wasn't my father. His seed gave me life. I never spoke with the man. Never met him though I saw him once from a distance long before I was told I had any connection to him."

An uneasy silence rippled between then. "He must have known who you were."

He shrugged. "I doubt it. Cabriotini didn't attempt to look for his bastards until he was dying. That's when he decided to find an heir."

She offered a thin smile. "He wanted you then."

Marco laughed, the bitter sound mirroring his dislike of his paternity. "Don't paint this into something homey. He detested the thought of leaving his wealth to a distant cousin in Majorca. So he hired investigators to discover if he'd sired any bastards in Italy." He gave a gruff snort. "Cabriotini's attorney hit the jackpot, finding my young sister and then me some months after the investigation was launched."

She winced, her burning cheeks surely as pink as the roses clustered against an ivory wall. "He must have been a very miserable man."

"Cabriotini lived hard and played hard and enjoyed a procession of mistresses. According to them, he made it clear to every women he bedded that he would deny any 'mistakes' that might evolve from a liaison." His mouth pulled into that pained smile again and she shifted away from the car door without realizing she'd done so.

Not that Marco noticed. His gaze was riveted out the window again, his broad shoulders so stiff she imagined them lashed to a steel girder.

She worried her lower lip, wanting to avoid a scene. God knew she'd endured enough of them in her life.

"You haven't been a family for very long then," she ventured, thinking by diverting the conversation to his sister again it could qualify a bit as her doing her job.

"We've never been a family," he said flatly.

"When did you become so cold, so unfeeling?"

"Ten years ago," he said, not even deigning to look at her.

She bit her lower lip and stared at her clasped hands, surprised they were trembling. Of course he would blame everything on that awful night when he'd cornered her and her father in the posh Zwuavé Gardens in Mayfair, accusing David Tate of stealing his family business, accusing Delanie of betraying him.

She'd never been able to forget that ugly scene. Each second of that confrontation was embedded in her memory, each hurtful word tattooed on her heart.

"How could you believe I betrayed you?" she asked as the car cruised down the poplar-lined driveway, taking her deeper into his lair.

Marco snorted, pressing a knuckled fist into the leather seat, accusing gaze drilling into her. "You were the only person I confided in about my grandmother's mental state. You knew I intended to remove her from her role in her own business before she was taken advantage of. You told your father this and he swooped down on her."

As she'd done that night, with her heart threatening to pound out of her chest, she shook her head in denial. "I never told Father anything."

Marco leaned closer and loomed over her. "Then how did he know something that I told only you?"

She shook her head, having no answer. Never in a million years would she have divulged what they'd spoken of in whispers, arms and legs entangled, bare bodies curled perfectly together in a delicious skin-on-skin rub. Their intimacy had been a precious gift to her. She wouldn't have jeopardized that.

But her father would, she admitted, worrying her bottom lip with her teeth, the same question plaguing her mind as well.

She'd been so wrong about this man, certain he loved her, certain he believed her innocence. Certain that he would return for her. But he'd disappeared.

When she'd needed him most, he'd proven to be no better than her father.

That night at the restaurant with Marco and David Tate she'd hardened, realizing with a sinking heart that her father had used her to get to Marco and he'd succeeded. He'd used the one good thing in her life against her—used his daughter.

"What did you do, Father?" she had demanded, ice crystallizing in her veins as she'd confronted her father, his light eyes devoid of any emotion.

"What did I do?" he parroted then laughed, a nasty cackle that taunted—haunted her still. "You know exactly what I did. As you well know, one learns so much through pillow talk."

The insinuation she'd intentionally betrayed the man she loved had her face flaming—not with shame but with anger. She'd known her father was the ultimate manipulator, but she'd never dreamed he would go to such lengths to best Marco.

A huge error on her part. Any man who beat his wife wasn't above using his daughter to his benefit.

"I didn't give you any information," she'd hissed, but her father only gave her that smug smile.

She'd only mentioned her worry over Marco's grandmother to one person: her own mother. But her mother wouldn't have divulged something Delanie told her in private. She wouldn't have betrayed her. Would she?

She'd turned to Marco ten years ago, standing at their table tall and proud and so very angry. "He's lying, Marco. I would never hurt you. Never betray you."

He'd stared at her a long time before he stepped closer, dragging one finger down her cheek that was slick with tears she hadn't realized she'd shed, his palm strong yet gentle as he cupped her chin. She leaned into that hand, her gaze on his, begging him to believe her.

"Then how could your father possibly know things that I shared only with you?" he asked, pulling his hand back, denying her his touch, his trust.

She shook her head, having no solid answer. "He spied on us. He must have."

The anger in his beautiful brown eyes cooled to a brittle glaze that chilled her to the bone. And she knew that the torrid love they'd shared was freezing over.

Marco had backed away from the table, the epitome of arrogant pride. And she held her breath, praying for him to see the truth, waiting for him to extend his hand to her.

Instead, he turned and walked away with brisk determined steps, spine straight, broad shoulders girded in an impossibly stiff line.

She'd pressed trembling fingers to her lips, stilling the cry that tried to escape. Rejection bludgeoned her and she shrank in her chair, humiliated. Stunned. Hurt beyond words.

"That was unpleasant," her father said, returning his attention to his beef Wellington and topped-off glass of port, dismissing her heartache as if it were nothing.

Because to her father, she was nothing. It had never been more clear to her than at that moment.

She pushed to her feet on shaky legs, the scrape of chair legs blaring over the din of happy customers.

"I hate you," she hissed, batting tears from her eyes.

Her father had lifted one sardonic brow then laughed, a dark sound edged with sarcasm. "Of course you do. Perhaps you should hurry after Mr. Vincienta. Beg him to take you back," he said. "I don't need you and neither does your mother."

But her mother did need her.

Delanie could see the retribution gathering in his light eyes and her stomach twisted into a tighter knot. She knew his pattern. He would need to release his tension over being confronted publicly by Marco and now her.

Her mother would pay the ultimate price. Again.

Even so she wove through the restaurant on shaky legs, mumbling excuses as she went, heart thundering in her chest. She had to speak with Marco one more time. She had to make him believe she'd had no part in her father's latest scheme. That she was as much a victim as anyone else.

"Marco!" she cried out as she pushed past the doorman and stumbled onto the sidewalk, her teary gaze frantically searching for him.

He stopped in the arc of light but didn't face her.

Heart in her throat, she gulped a sob and raced to him. Her trembling fingers banded his arm and he stiffened even more.

"I don't know how he found out about your grandmother but I was ignorant of his plan. I played no part in his corporate schemes," she said. "You have to believe me."

He looked at her then with an expression so cold she shivered. "No, I do not have to believe you."

She batted at a tear that leaked from her gritty eyes only to do the same with another. And another. She gave up the effort to stay them and looked at him through a veil of tears.

"I've never told a soul since primary school, but you have to know the truth. Father is abusive," she said.

His brows snapped together. "To you?"

She shook her head and gulped in great drafts of air. "To Mother. He's always abused her, though he was careful her bruises didn't show." Until that last time…

Her fingers inched up his rigid forearm. "I can't leave her. He'll—" She shook her head again, fingers digging into his muscled arm. "I don't know what depths he will sink to this time if I defy him again."

"You're telling the truth?" he asked, his frown fierce.

"Yes," she whispered past dry lips.

"You need to escape his grasp. Come with me to Italy."

When he'd asked her before, in the heat of passion, she'd refused because, while he'd told her he wanted her, he'd never professed his love. He always held back something she couldn't define, she'd just sensed the wall going up. That kept her from totally trusting him as she longed to do.

But now he was giving her a real chance to escape her

hellish life. To be with the man she loved, the man with the wounded heart that she still believed her love could heal. She wanted to go but wouldn't unless specific conditions were met.

"Yes, I'll go with you but not without my mother. I can't leave her to suffer." The guilt of doing so once still plagued her. "Please. I love you, Marco. I need your help. I need you."

Marco jerked his head aside, his rigid posture concealing anything he was feeling. And she'd prayed he believed her. Prayed that he would help her and her mother.

"Go back to your father but say nothing about telling me this," he said. "I'll go to your house now and speak with your mother. Trust me to arrange everything. It will be all right."

She'd swallowed hard. Trust was asking so much, especially with so much at stake. Especially when she was leery of putting her heart and soul into his hands. But she loved him. She wanted to believe he would never hurt her but she needed time—time she simply didn't have.

"Okay," she said. "When will I see you?"

"Soon."

He stood there a moment longer, staring into her eyes before his gaze fixed on her mouth. *Kiss me,* she thought. *Hold me. Convince me everything will be fine. Perfect. Make the fear go away.*

But he did none of that.

In a blink he disappeared into the darkness, leaving her with the unpleasant task of trudging back into the restaurant and facing her father.

"Did you change your mind about leaving with the Italian or did he reject you?" her father asked the moment she eased onto the chair across from him.

She damned the heat flooding her cheeks and averted her eyes so he wouldn't read the truth in them. "He was already gone by the time I got outside."

"Hmm," her father said, cradling his port in one pale hand,

the long slender fingers looking too effeminate to be capable of inflicting pain.

But she knew differently.

As Marco had asked of her, she suffered the evening in her father's company. Her nerves jumped like live wires by the time they returned home but she held onto the belief he would make everything right. That she and her mother would soon be free.

She hurried to her mother's room, hoping Marco had talked over a plan with her. That they would be leaving here soon. That they would finally be free of David Tate's control.

"Well? What did Marco say? When do we leave?" Delanie asked in hushed tones.

Small furrows raced across her mother's pale forehead, the skin so thin and white it was nearly translucent. "I've no idea what you're talking about."

And so Delanie explained it in a rush, her fragile faith in Marco withering when her mother gave her a pitying smile. "He never came, dear. He never called."

"But he said—"

"Men are the kings of false promises," her mother interrupted, her fragile blue-veined hand patting Delanie's in a conciliatory gesture that failed to comfort. "You should know that by now."

Yes, she should know it. Did know it. But she'd begun to trust Marco.

"Mother, did you ever mention what I told you about Marco's grandmother?" she asked.

"No, not a word," her mother said, but looked everywhere but at her. "Why do you ask?"

Delanie waved a dismissive hand. "Just curious. It's just that I told nobody but you and yet Father has learned of it."

Her mother had smiled. "You should know by now that the walls here have ears."

Yes, of course. A maid must have overheard and told

someone. That's how the information had trickled back to her father.

Delanie had gone to her room that night, refusing to sob. Tears solved nothing. She'd crawled into bed and curled into a ball, vowing never to fall victim to love and a man's control again.

Yet, ten years later, here she was as the car stopped under the portico of the palatial villa, blinking eyes that burned with unshed tears. Heart aching in an all too familiar pain that she thought she had buried long ago.

A glance at the tall Italian who'd just pushed out of the auto gave her the answer.

Years ago Marco had simply stormed out of her life, turning her tenuous trust in him to dust as he walked over the shards of her broken heart. Now he was back, causing her to doubt her mother's loyalty. Making her want to lean on him all over again. The odd pang in her chest confirmed the one thing she'd feared most. She was still vulnerable to Marco's magnetic charm. Still not over him.

This time she would guard her heart.

Marco stood a moment stretching his long legs. His gaze climbed the gray walls of Cabriotini's Italianate villa, the red tile roof gleaming in the late-afternoon sun and the well-tended lawn with artistically designed flower beds overflowing with bright yellow and orange blossoms.

His time living here was about over. Two weeks and he would move to his home. In two weeks he wouldn't be haunted by the stigma of this villa. Or by Delanie Tate?

The hint of a smile tugged at his lips as he rounded the hood. He opened her door and extended a hand, challenging her to accept his manners or publicly snub him.

There was a long pause as she sat huddled on the plush seat, sunlight dancing down the length of her lovely legs encased in the sheerest hose, the skin pale. Were they still as smooth?

Sexy legs. That was the first thing he'd noticed about her before discovering how luscious the whole package was—full breasts, lush, inviting lips, soft, yielding body begging for sex.

"We manage a sparse staff," he said, dragging his gaze back to hers. "But they'll see that your reasonable needs are met."

"I don't need or wish to be waited on," she said, slipping her small hand in his and exiting with the grace befitting quality.

"It's breathtaking," Delanie said, her silken wrap slipping down her arms as she extracted her hand from his.

He just caught himself from grabbing the shawl. From easing it around her narrow shoulders and stealing a caress.

"Yes, breathtaking," he said, his gaze on her.

Her face was uplifted to the sun, one hand shielding her eyes, her golden hair fluttering in the warm breeze scented with ripe fruit. Both were slightly sweet. Intoxicating.

His stomach tightened another notch, but fighting it was as useless as trying to ignore it.

Delanie Tate was still the most beautiful woman he'd ever met. Still stirred something in him that he hadn't truly understood himself. That he couldn't control.

Oh, there was attraction. Lust even. But the odd feelings churning deep inside him went beyond that.

She took him to a level he didn't understand. Didn't trust.

Hell, he couldn't trust her to abide by her word. Which is why he had to keep her close. Had to make sure she planned his sister's wedding right down to the last canapé and curled bit of ribbon, that she saw it through to the end.

She looked at him then, cheeks pink from the sun, lush lips holding a tentative smile.

He sucked in a breath, ignoring the urge to drag her into his arms. Hold her. Kiss her.

"You won't miss living here, will you?" she asked.

"Not one bit. I look forward to moving into my home." He motioned to the door. "After you."

She studied him a moment longer before striding toward the door. He took a breath and followed, keeping his gaze trained on her glorious hair instead of her inviting backside.

"Will you continue to keep in close contact with your sister or are you ready to push her out of your life as well?" she asked.

"Why the concern?" he shot back.

She stopped at the door and faced him. "You've made it clear you have never been a family man and yet you've lived in a place you dislike for years. Now you've gone to the trouble to force me here to plan your sister's wedding." Her gaze locked with his. "Why do all that? And don't spout duty!"

He rubbed the bridge of his nose and heaved a sigh. She couldn't know how much he wanted to rid himself of this place or why. How reluctant he was to open his heart to Bella—the sister who was a stranger in so many ways.

All his life he'd tried to be a good grandson. A good son. A good man to one good woman—Delanie.

But in the end he hadn't been good enough for any of them. His aged grandmother had trusted a stranger over him. His mother had let him live a lie and his biological father had shunned him.

And Delanie…

Delanie had betrayed his trust. His love. And yet she still plagued his thoughts over the years.

The one who got away, he thought with a mocking smile. Only that wasn't the truth.

Sobering, looking at her now standing before him so proud and vexed, he could only admit the truth. She was the one he'd pushed away. Ruthlessly. Furiously.

Wisest thing he'd ever done or biggest mistake of his life? That question nagged at him at the oddest times, but he'd never been more determined to discern the truth until now.

To do that he needed to spend time alone with Delanie.

"It's not Bella I wish to distance myself from," he said at

last, his eyes never leaving hers. "It's this place. It symbolizes a pattern of life that I fell into naturally, just like the man who sired me."

She stared at him through narrowed eyes, mouth drawn in a tight bow. "You were following in your father's footsteps?"

He gave a curt nod, the admission coming hard. "I was certainly headed that direction after the collapse of my business. Cabriotini's death changed that pattern of life. Changed me."

"For the better?"

"That depends on who you ask," he said. "Come. I'm sure you would like to find your room and rest."

"Actually I'd like to meet your sister first. The sooner I can get started formulating plans for her wedding the better."

Not what he expected to hear but he had no objections. Bella could be another matter.

"Of course."

He asked the housekeeper to summon his sister then led Delanie into the salon awash with sunlight thanks to a bank of tall windows. The French doors had been thrown open to the patio, admitting a warm welcoming breeze sweetened with the spice of ripe grapes.

Yet the only scent teasing his senses to distraction was the floral one wafting around Delanie. She was still in his blood, but where he really wanted her was in his bed, willing and hot for him.

Soon, he thought as he crossed to the liquor cabinet. "Would you care for a drink?"

Definitely, but dulling her senses around Marco could be a huge error on her part. More than ever she needed to keep her wits sharp. If she ignored the sudden sexual overtones radiating from him then just maybe she could muddle through being close to him.

Still, she heard herself ask, "Is it one of your labels?"

"Our premiere sagrantino," he said, handing her a glass of glistening torrid red wine. "Eight years old and entering its

prime. Or would you prefer something less robust? A mer-
lot perhaps?"

"No, the sagrantino will be fine."

She took the glass from him, careful not to touch his fingers, careful not to find too much significance in that remark.
It was no surprise that he remembered her favorite wine. It
stood to reason that her adversary would use something she
liked to lull her.

Adversary... Her eyes flicked to Marco's dark enigmatic
ones and she suddenly couldn't breathe, couldn't do anything
but clutch the fine stem of the glass between her fingers.

She ran her tongue over her lips as the intensity in his eyes
burned her from the inside out, the heat so strong she feared
he would devour her.

This awareness between them had always been there.
Always had been strong. But even knowing that hadn't prepared her for the onslaught of emotions. She'd been so sure
anger at him would kill her desire. But it hadn't.

"To Bella's wedding," he said, raising his glass.

A trickle of awareness skipped up her arms and legs and
she shifted, edgy, needy, instantly aware of the change in him.
Was this how a hare felt being stalked?

She stiffened but lifted her glass to his, the melodic ting
of crystal resonating in the air while a different awareness
played over her nerves, leaving them humming.

"Yes, to your sister's wedding," she said, well aware he was
the master of manipulation when it came to her.

He drank, the bronzed column of his throat working, the
seductive bow of his lips stained by the dark wine. She stared,
unable to move, to do anything but remember a time when
they'd found a secluded glen and come together, drinking red
wine from cheap glasses and each other.

Her skin tightened at the memory of him laving it off her
body with his tongue. How his eyes had locked with hers, blazing with heat and lust and what she'd thought was love. He'd

thrust into her deeply that day, making them one, making her feel whole and cherished and loved for the first time in her life.

"Are you sure you wouldn't prefer a different wine?" he asked, breaking the spell that held her as tightly as chains.

She flicked him a smile, hands thankfully steady on the wineglass. "No, I was just tangled in thoughts."

"About?"

About what could have been if they hadn't splintered apart.

Wasted energy. Nothing could come of them together again, but that didn't calm the deep hum that vibrated through her, hot and thrumming with a pulse that was so needy. Even knowing he'd never loved her, she had never been able to forget him. Never had been able to think of letting another man touch her.

She would surely never trust so easily again.

"I was thinking about all I need to do." She swirled the dark wine before taking a sip.

Her senses exploded to life while the alcohol went straight to her head. Just like the man staring at her giving her that bubbly, fuzzy feeling that coursed through her veins.

"Lovely," she got out a bit breathlessly.

"I am glad you like it." He moved closer, almost prying her glass from her stiff fingers then backing her up against the sun-warmed expanse of wall oh so easily. "The fruity taste lingers on the tongue while the tart acidity awakens the palate, don't you think?"

He was going to kiss her. She read it in the dark smoky glint of his eyes. Sensed it in his obviously aroused body pressing close to hers. And, God help her, she wanted that kiss. Wanted his mouth on hers, his hands stroking her body.

Her heart raced like the wind and her mind spun in a bizarre panic. She couldn't let it happen and yet that's exactly what she wanted him to do. Kiss her. Mold her to his length.

"Our relationship is strictly business," she said, clapping a palm against the steely wall of his chest, desperate to stop this, to avoid a repeat of history that would fling her right back into the hot swirling depths of consuming passion.

"It can be whatever we wish," he said, stepping so close her scent swirled about him like silken scarves.

"No. You're wrong."

She held her ground, looking up at him with eyes that had known pain, known heartache. One night long ago he'd glimpsed the beginnings of that grief and believed it, got lost in her need and his own. He wasn't gullible now.

Yet instinct told him that what he read in her eyes was real. This was a reflection of pain learned one way—by experience.

"Why so wary?" he asked. "I've abided by all you asked."

"I've had little cause to trust anyone."

Hadn't they both? "A lesson learned from your father?"

Her chin came up, her gaze frosting. "And from you."

He flinched as the salvo struck his heart. "How can I possibly be blamed for your distrust?"

Dammit, were those tears in her eyes? No matter. He wouldn't let them influence him again.

Ten years ago he'd fallen for her sob story until the truth had won out. It was a painful reminder of how devious a woman could be, a lesson learned from his mother's infidelity.

Nothing learned in his recent investigation of Delanie swayed him to believe her now. She'd tricked him, betrayed him...

"You said you would come for me," she said. "You promised to help me and my mother. But you lied."

His fingers tightened on the glass until they numbed. That was the last thing he expected her to bring up.

"No, that most certainly wasn't a lie," he said.

"Then why didn't you come for me? Why didn't you call?"

Because he'd found her out to be the liar. The one using him in a new way. Yet now he had trouble dredging up that same level of distrust. He found himself questioning what had once seemed so clear.

He drove his fingers through his hair, hating this sense of uncertainty. Is this a hell similar to that his own father had lived with? That had left Marco feeling isolated as a teen? Abandoned? Unloved?

"Papa, why do you ignore me? Why do you and Mama argue all the time?" he'd asked soon after they'd moved to Umbria.

"Ignore you? I'm a busy man," his father had said. "Ask your mother why we are like this," his father would say.

And when Marco had, his mother would burst into tears.

Just as Delanie had when confronted with her betrayal.

Yes, revenge had sounded sweeter than the succulent sagrantino grapes ripening in his vineyard to Marco. He'd lived for this moment. Planned it well. But the reality of forcing Delanie to do his bidding tasted as bitter as fruit harvested far too soon.

The impulse to touch her was too strong. Too overwhelming to ignore. He brushed back errant strands of hair that looked and felt like silk, careful not to touch her skin. Careful not to spook her.

"I did come, Delanie," he said. "I made arrangements to spirit you both away and met with your mother as I'd promised. But when I offered her sanctuary she refused."

"No. Mum wouldn't have done that."

He ground his teeth. If this were a man continually calling him a liar... But it wasn't. It was Delanie, the sweetly feminine thorn in his side.

"Believe what you will," he said, well aware she would anyway.

She set her glass down and pressed both palms to her temples. "This makes no sense. Father abused her. Why would she refuse the chance to escape that life?"

"Your mother denied everything you told me," he said, his eyes boring into her suddenly startled ones.

"No!"

He shrugged. "It's the truth."

And Delanie looked into his eyes and knew it was so. He'd come for her and her mother. But her mum had sworn to her that Marco had never come. Never called.

The last bastion of her childhood crumbled before her eyes into dust, clinging, choking, leaving a remnant of deceit that couldn't be easily wiped away.

That night she'd believed her mother, her confidant. While her heart had been breaking, it had never crossed her mind once that her mother would do anything to harm her. Deceive her.

Delanie pressed trembling fingers to her temples where a headache threatened to pound to life, sickened by the truth that loomed before her. Had the mother she'd sacrificed her own freedom for betrayed her confidence? Used her?

The walls have ears, her mother had told her whenever she would question how her father knew of her plans. And she'd believed her mother, she admitted, hands falling to her sides.

Poor naive fool, she chided herself.

My God, her mother had been the one who'd alerted David Tate to Marco's ailing grandmother. *She'd* told him about Delanie's plans and concerns for her own company, setting the stage to halt her independence. Her mother had stolen her chance of happiness with Marco, all because she would not leave the abusive husband she loved and whose horrific temper she constantly made excuses for.

"I don't know who or what to believe anymore," she said, turning to the window, more confused and hurt and angry than she'd ever been in her life.

"It's difficult when lies are buried among the truths."

So true. It was glaringly clear that both her parents had manipulated and lied to her all her life. Her trust in her mother had made it so easy to play into her father's hands. To give him control over her future while destroying Marco's legacy.

This truth cut deep and bled.

She cast him a quick look then glanced away, unable to meet his steady gaze for long, afraid she would see pity in his eyes. "I don't have the heart even to try anymore."

"It's not like you to give up."

Strong hands cupped her shoulders. His offer of support?

God knew she desperately needed a strong shoulder to lean on now. But Marco? He'd betrayed her as well. He could be using her now.

She shrugged him off and scooted aside, heart thundering and skin tingling. "Don't touch me. Please."

"Cara—"

"Am I interrupting a private moment?" a woman asked, her tone holding a hint of amusement.

Delanie stared at the women. She was young and pretty, though the petulant bow to her mouth and the annoying snap of masticating chewing gum kept her from being a raving beauty or an ingénue.

"My sister, Bella," he introduced.

"Delanie Tate," she said.

The younger woman flashed a wide smile. "Good. You're finally here. I'm about to go out of my mind dealing with these old traditionalists."

Delanie flicked a look at Marco but he merely shrugged. It was the first time she'd seen him look uncertain.

She faced the bride. "I gather you would prefer a modern wedding."

Bella bobbed her head. "Heavens, yes. It's a joke for me to wear virginal white."

Heat burned Delanie's cheeks, but she continued smiling and jumped at the chance to get through this crucial meeting with Bella now. Once she knew the young woman's wants she could get to work on a proposal. Far away from Marco Vincienta.

"Please, let's sit and talk," Delanie said, motioning to the seating area where a sumptuous cream sofa was flanked by overstuffed chairs. "What are your preferences as to color?"

Bella slumped onto a stripped chair, pulling her bare feet beneath her. "Pale blue." She frowned. "Or green."

"Both are lovely choices," Delanie said as she took her electronic notebook from her purse and eased onto the sofa close to Bella, ready to fill the blanks in on her unique form. "With your dark coloring, you would look stunning in either though the green would truly bring out the gold flecks in your dark eyes."

Eyes that were strikingly similar to Marco's. They must have their father's eyes, she surmised, though she refrained from saying that aloud.

"I would love that," Bella gushed.

A glance at Marco found him watching his sister, dark brows drawn over his classic nose and muscular arms locked over his broad chest. Delanie had expected impatience but he seemed as interested in what his sister said as Delanie.

She shook off the distraction that was solely Marco with a discreet cough, vowing to ignore him. "I gather you'd like nontraditional flowers as well?"

Bella nodded. "Anything but roses or calla lilies or anything else that someone has declared as symbolizing everlasting love."

Ah, that was a telling remark if she ever heard one. But she didn't press the point now with Marco watching them like a hawk.

She was here to please his sister. Not him. He'd already told her money was no object.

Delanie made a few notes, already having an idea of an avenue to pursue. "Where will the ceremony be held?"

"The cathedral in the village," Marco said.

"No! I will marry in St. Antonio de Montiforte or not at all," Bella said.

An uneasy tension pulsed between the siblings. Delanie

cleared her throat, having dealt with similar matters in the past.

She faced Marco. "You hired me to plan a wedding that would please your sister, to do as she wishes. That means that she decides where to exchange her vows. Correct?"

Marco mumbled something, likely a curse. "Fine. Have the wedding in Montiforte. Force your guests to drive an hour to your wedding and back here for the reception. Unless you have changed your mind about that as well!"

"We want to hold the reception in Castello di Montiforte," Bella said.

Marco scrubbed a hand over his mouth and shifted, and for a moment Delanie almost felt sorry for him having two women tear down his plans. But his refusal to believe her still rose like a wall between them, bolstering her determination to keep her distance from him.

He heaved a sigh. "Perhaps since the gardens are less than perfect it is best to hold the reception there."

"I knew you would understand," Bella said, then smiled such a serene smile that Delanie nearly laughed.

Marco snorted but kept his thoughts to himself.

In short order, Delanie went over a few more points to ensure she had no doubts as to the bride's preferences.

"That should do it," Delanie said. "I'll contact you if I have any questions. And please, if you want anything changed, no matter how insignificant it seems, let me know right away."

"I will." Bella clapped her hands together and rose. "Thank you for agreeing to plan my wedding after all."

"Thank your brother," Delanie said. "He convinced me to travel here."

Bella squealed and ran to her brother, throwing her arms around him with a hug that looked comfortable. "Marco, *grazie!* It will be perfect now. Oh! I must tell my fiancé. You will take care of Miss Tate?"

"Very good care." He gaze flicked to Delanie, his smile going from brotherly to something knowing and hot.

A zillion butterflies took flight in her stomach and she pressed a hand to her middle before taking a breath. She couldn't stay here at the villa while she was planning a wedding that was taking place an hour away. She couldn't stay anywhere near Marco without having to battle her desire every moment.

"I have a tremendous amount to do in short order," she said as she stuffed her electronic notebook back in her purse. "Which is why I must relocate to Montiforte. "

"You're serious?"

"Very." She rose and faced him, and damned her suddenly weak knees. It simply wasn't fair that he had this effect on her. "I would appreciate it if your driver would take me there now so I can get settled in. I want to start early in the morning with the arrangements."

He crossed his arms over his chest and lifted one mocking brow. "Why do I have the feeling you are anxious to get away from me?"

"I'm sure I wouldn't know. The driver?"

"I sent him home for the night."

"Then I'll ring for a cab."

"That isn't necessary."

She slapped her hands on her hips and fumed. "I suppose you have a better idea?"

His widening smile was a sensual promise that every nerve in her body recognized and responded to with a quickening sizzle through her blood. "Of course, *cara*. I'll take you to Montiforte and personally see you settled in."

CHAPTER FIVE

EMOTIONS whirled like a vortex within Delanie, leaving her shaking. Being in Marco's company for another hour was the last thing she wanted. But suffering the sexual allure of his body again was preferable to staying in this villa with him in residence, knowing he was just down the hall.

If only she could fully trust that she would walk away from this in total control of her business. But she couldn't.

Her father had used her. If Marco had told the truth, then her mother had lied. Even then, there was the fact that Marco refused to believe her.

She bit her lower lip, trying to get entranced by the ribbons of sun streaming over the undulating hills. If only she could find more appeal in this sunset instead of the man beside her.

Impossible to do with him behind the wheel of the powerful red sports car. Ferrari? Bugatti? She hadn't a clue.

No matter how hard she tried, her gaze kept flicking back to his hands on the leather-wrapped wheel. Hands that she remembered all too well coaxing oh-too-ready responses from her body with equal ease.

"You will have absolute privacy here," he said.

Twilight bathed the hills in shades of amber and crimson by the time they reached the walled hamlet of Montiforte. An ancient castle dominated one end of town and an equally aged church filled the other.

In between rose a collection of oddly shaped buildings, some standing nearly atop the other. All faced a small square piazza where a lichen-covered god stood on an equally aged stepped pedestal next to an old well.

"I didn't expect Montiforte to be so small and medieval," she said.

"It is one of the oldest settlements in Umbria. Come, the village market is still open. You will need supplies at the villa."

She climbed out before he could assist her this time and walked with him to the lone shop. The sweet fragrance of ripe grapes hung in the air, but Marco's spicy scent dominated. Just like the man.

The shopkeeper greeted him by name, but the rest was lost to her as they lapsed into a rapid flow of Italian. She took the time while they visited to wander around the small shop.

The savory smells were feasts in themselves. Balls, ropes and small wheels of cheese hung amid an array of sausages.

Canted tables held an assortment of fresh fruits and vegetables. She leaned over a baker's case filled with baguettes, fat rounds of breads and a selection of rolls. One round loaf caught her eye.

"The *torta di testo* is delicious toasted and drizzled with olive oil," Marco said, standing beside her holding two cheeses and a string of sausage. "It is good for sandwiches as well."

The shopkeeper nodded and brought out a basket filled with the round flat bread. His smile encouraged her to choose.

"Thank you," she said, selecting several and trying not to recall a similar day outside London when she and Marco had stopped in a shop for a takeaway lunch, deciding spontaneously to turn it into a picnic instead.

And they'd feasted the better part of the day on sweets and savories and hot kisses, getting more intoxicated on each other than on the wine. One look at him now was proof he could do so again.

A hot swirl of heat curled low in her belly and she frowned, annoyed her thoughts always splintered off into something torrid with him. It would be so easy to fall into his arms, his bed.

But with pleasure came heartache. She'd learned that lesson well. Even the unspoken promise of pleasure she glimpsed in his eyes could turn on her like a viper.

"This is really more than enough," she said.

"Who knows? You may have company."

Like him? Her throat went dry at the thought of entertaining Marco in a villa, just the two of them. There had been a time when she would have done anything to get him alone.

"I'm sure I'll be far too busy working to receive guests," she said, pulling out her wallet to pay for her purchases.

"Meals are included in your contract," he said, giving the shopkeeper a look that had the man turning from her.

There wasn't a thing in the contract regarding meals and they both knew it, but again arguing would only raise another passion. Best to let that issue rest.

She was already tired from the journey and stressed to the max by being with Marco again. "Thank you then."

Outside her gaze drifted over the stone buildings and narrow streets and walkways rising like steps up the hillside. There was just enough sun to give the village a Monet aura with bluing shadows creeping over stucco washed a mellow gold by the setting sun.

"There is a bistro near the castle that serves amazing food," he said as he joined her, his shadow swallowing her whole much as she knew his passion would do if she surrendered to it. "I suggest we eat before you retire to your residence."

And wouldn't that be cozy? Her sharing an intimate meal with the man she still found far too desirable.

She diverted her eyes from the magnetic draw of his. "I'm far too weary from the journey to enjoy it. Besides I have ample food to sustain me should I get hungry."

Over the thud of her own heart she heard the melodic strains of a mandolin, the music floating on a cooling breeze.

But she felt no chill, not with Marco standing so close, not when his nearness warmed her from the inside out.

"Very well then," he said. "Another time."

Not if she could avoid it.

He pressed a hand to her back and she swallowed a gasp as heat flooded her, spiraling out from his splayed fingers to flow through her in sultry waves. No, she had to keep her distance from this man who was already taking far too many liberties.

She hurried to the car and climbed in, not waiting for him to assist her. He hissed a curse and closed the door after her, and she took a breath then another as he walked around the front of the car, one strong, well-boned hand riding the sleek hood.

In moments he threw himself behind the wheel and they were off, the car winding up the hills lined with poplar and flanked by fields of grapes, their leaves a burnished gold hiding grapes that looked black this time of day.

Marco handled the powerful car with ease, seeming so arrogantly sure of himself that her nerves tightened another notch. She was no match for him. Never had been.

How funny that he accused her of betraying him, using him, when she'd been the vulnerable one, caught up in the magnetic pull of the dashing Italian. In the span of several weeks, he'd romanced her and proposed marriage.

While she desperately waited for him to come for her, he'd deserted her without explanation. Left her to believe her family's lies.

She'd lost her heart and her will to trust in love again. Lost control of her company and her life. Regaining it had became her goal. Her only vow was to avoid Marco should their paths ever cross again.

Yet here she was with him again, trying valiantly to subdue the stirrings of need inside her. She searched for gaping holes in everything he told her yet found nothing more than shadowed valleys.

She wanted to hate him, but her heart wouldn't let her. So

she hated herself for her inability to get over him, for not purging him from her system long ago.

"We're here." He stopped the car in front of a villa bathed in a burnished gold swath of sunset.

Her stomach tightened. "Is this a bed and breakfast?"

"No." His shirt glowed white with the sleeves rolled up and his tanned muscular forearms bared. "It is a private villa above Montiforte."

"A rental then?" she asked, thinking the fee must be exorbitant and glad she didn't have to pay the cost.

"It is yours for your stay here."

He extracted himself from behind the wheel with predatory grace and she stole a deep breath to steady her nerves, her entire body surrendering to a tremble as she blew it out. The trunk opened and closed, jarring her to move. But her door opened just as her hand was reaching for it.

She stared up into his eyes that were darker than sin and for the life of her she couldn't speak, couldn't move.

His hand reached for her and she froze, forgetting to breathe. "I won't bite."

Ah, but he had. Delicious nibbles along her limbs that she remembered with sensual clarity.

For the second time she placed her hand in his and left the car. Thankfully he let go of her first, reaching for the bag of groceries she clutched in one hand.

"I've got it," she said, stepping back.

He stared at her another moment before he motioned to the villa, his teeth wickedly white in the fading light. "Let's get you settled. A housekeeper comes twice a week. She'll be in tomorrow morning."

"Thanks for the warning."

Her skin tingled, nerves pinging wildly as she marched up the winding walk to the arched door. What was the matter with her that she couldn't squash thoughts of them entangled?

It was over. Done. She was here to do a job. Nothing more.

Her fingers closed around the antique brass knob but the door was locked. He reached around her to work a key into the lock, his spicy scent enveloping her and sending her senses on another spiraling jolt.

She turned, thinking to scoot away and give him room to open the door. Instead he caged her in with an arm to the door at her back and his hard unyielding length at her front.

His warm breath fanned her cheek and she bit back a moan. "Back off."

"No way."

His teeth flashed in a wolf's smile a heartbeat before he claimed her mouth with a possessive hunger that sparked a firestorm in her blood, that flung her right back to when Marco had first swept into her life like a hot tropical storm and spun her static existence on its head.

Distantly she heard a muffled thump. Her bag? She didn't know. Didn't care.

His arms banded around her, hauling her close, molding her to his length. His gaze burned into hers, melting her resolve. Every nerve in her body came awake, snapping and sizzling.

She wanted his kiss even though she knew it was wrong of her, even though she knew it could throw open the door to old pain. Her palms pressed against the unforgiving wall of his chest, but instead of shoving him away, they relearned the impressive contours of toned muscles.

His kiss commanded. Consumed. Her rigid admonition to keep him at arm's length caught fire and burned to ash as her fingers splayed, exploring the breadth of the man who haunted her dreams.

He was broader, more muscled, more dominant than before. More arrogantly male than any man she'd ever met, but she couldn't find the strength or reason to resist him, couldn't do anything but press against him and return his kisses with a matching heat, like a flower unfurling its petals to the glory of the sun.

One hand held her head just so, fingers threaded through her hair while the other stroked down her side, grazing the side of her breast, the dip of her waist and flare of her hip, setting off sensations she'd hadn't felt in too long.

She stirred, restless for him to do more than tease. To slip a hand between her thighs and ease the ache building inside her to the point she feared she would explode.

But he did nothing more than hold her tight and plumb the cay of her mouth. The spicy taste of him on her tongue was a delicious bubble that fizzed through her blood like champagne.

And popped as he pulled away, his smile smug. Victorious.

Why shouldn't he be since he'd beaten down her defenses with little effort?

Her face burned but her body chilled. She pushed away from him and stormed inside, whirling to face him, fingers taking a punishing grip on the open door.

"Leave me be, Marco. Get it through your head that I want nothing to do with you."

Near-black eyes drilled into her, his desire evident. "Then why did you kiss me?"

"Consider it a weak moment that won't happen again," she said. It could lead nowhere but to more hurt for her because she wasn't one who could have an affair without emotions. "I'm here to do a job. Not to delve into casual sex with a former lover."

He smirked. "You could have fooled me."

She hiked her chin up and shoved the door shut, refusing to dignify that remark. All she wanted now was privacy so she could sort through the tangle of emotions tugging at her.

He caught the heavy panel before it arced halfway and pushed it wide. "We aren't done yet."

"I disagree. Now please leave so I can focus on your sister's wedding, or have you forgotten that's why you forced me to come here?" She swept up her bag of groceries and stormed into the salon, hoping the kitchen lay through the wide arched opening ahead.

Her instincts were right, amazing considering the steady thud of his steps on the terra-cotta tiles that should have sent her running. Despite the dark open-beamed ceilings, the villa was surprisingly light, the kitchen especially so thanks to arched double doors that opened onto the terrace to let the last rays of the setting sun arrow through their multi-paned glass panels.

"I have not forgotten," he said, his voice so close that she knew he was right on her heels.

She placed her bag from the market on the large brick bar topped with the same warm terra-cotta tiles and whirled to face him. "Then please, leave me in peace."

His lips pulled into a thin line, but it was the windows slamming down on his desire at the same time as rigidity stole over his features that fascinated her. He looked every inch the unforgiving ruthless businessman.

To think she'd been so close to letting him command her body again. Far too close to risk being in his company much longer.

"How long do you really think you can go on denying what we both want?" he asked.

"Forever," she shot back.

He straightened and crossed his arms over his chest. "You will change your mind."

Damn his arrogance! Damn it that he was right! If she spent much time with him she would crumble into his arms, into his bed. That kiss had proved just how weak she was around him.

That admission shamed her. Hadn't the pain of having her father and then Marco betray her been enough?

And if he was telling the truth? If Mother did lie to him that night, sending him away with the belief that Delanie had been in league with her father?

She shook her head. What did it matter? True love wouldn't dissolve at the first sign of trouble.

Marco should have believed her. He should have returned to her, confronting her with what her mother had said, because if he had…

She would have left with Marco that night. She wouldn't have wasted the last ten years of her life.

If she could believe Marco…

"I won't change my mind," she said, painfully aware she couldn't turn back the hands of time, that she couldn't regain what had been lost.

He deposited her overnight bag on the terra-cotta floor, his gaze riveted on her. A few feet separated them but the magnetic pull between them was just as strong as ever.

"We'll see," he said, the firm lips that had ravished hers curving in a knowing smile.

That's all it took to set off a deep quiver that arced between her hipbones and mocked her ability to refuse him for long. They both knew her mind could say no but her body was a traitor, wanting him still.

She grabbed her overnight case and stormed toward the back of the house, hoping she would find a bedroom with a solid door. "Thank you for arranging for me to stay here. You know the way out."

That was met with silence which didn't surprise her. She just prayed he would leave, that he wouldn't remain here to tear down the already shaky wall surrounding her defenses.

Escape through the first door to the right seemed most prudent. She closed it behind her and ran home the old-fashioned bolt to keep Marco out.

And then, finally, she took a deep quivery breath and sagged against the door. The bag slipped from her hands and dropped. She closed her eyes and listened.

A lifetime seemed to pass before she heard the purr of a powerful engine. It had to be Marco leaving as she'd asked, though the only way to know would be to return to the dining area.

She grabbed her bag and pushed away from the door, then simply stared at the huge bed that dominated the room. A bit much for a rental and far larger than what she needed, but she wasn't about to complain.

Once she'd put her change of clothes in a dresser drawer, she ventured back into the dining area. The house was quiet with one lamp on in the salon. Nobody was here but her and her lingering memories.

Still, she opened the front door and stepped out onto the terrace, scanning the area shrouded in shadows. Lights winked at her from the village below, but there was no sign of Marco's flashy red car.

He'd left.

She trudged inside and secured the locks on the door, then moved to the ones off the dining area and did the same. A yawn slipped from her followed by another.

When had she eaten last? She couldn't remember. Her stomach had been in too tight a coil on the flight to risk food. Now she was simply too tired.

She needed sleep, but first needed to deal with the food she'd bought. Or Marco had bought. Did it matter at this stage?

It took a moment to put the fresh vegetables and fruit on a plate. Another to slip the cheese and sausage into the refrigerator.

That already had food in it? She blinked. Straightened.

Was this an added service like posh hotels? You pay for what you use? Or forgotten items from the last renter?

She shook her head and let loose another yawn. It was a matter she could deal with tomorrow.

Moments later she secluded herself in the big bed, on the verge of exhaustion. A muffled sound threatened to snap her out of it, but the sleep pulling at her was too great for her to stay alert.

Quiet. All was quiet. The doors were locked. Marco was gone from the house. She hoped he would be absent from her dreams as well this night.

The decisive closing of a door brought Delanie wide awake. She sat up in the sumptuous bed and blinked, stunned that the sun was already up.

The echo of footsteps on the tiles drifted to her. She tensed. Alert. Someone else was in the villa.

It took a moment for her mind to clear. It must be the housekeeper Marco had mentioned.

She let out the breath she'd sucked in and headed for the en suite facilities. A quick shower would wash away the last dregs of sleep, a necessity since she did need to get started planning Bella's wedding today.

With luck her path would rarely cross a certain arousing Italian's for the next two weeks. Now if she could just keep him from intruding on her thoughts.

After giving her hair a quick towel-drying, she dressed in black jeans, a turquoise jersey and sandals.

By the time she had her morning tea and fruit, her fine hair would be dry and she could set off to the center of Montiforte. With luck she could hitch a ride with the housekeeper.

An afternoon spent in the village would be the ideal time for her to combine personal shopping with a brief investigation of what was readily available there. When she was exhausted, she could either rent an auto or hire a cab to drive her back to the villa.

The second she stepped into the kitchen, awash in sunlight, she saw the housekeeper busy dusting in the salon. A plate of flaky pastries were set out on the kitchen bar with a jar of some dark berry jam beside them.

Her mouth watered and the hollow pang in her stomach confirmed she'd gone far too long without food. But then, she'd been too upset on the flight even to think about eating.

"Good morning," she greeted as she stepped into the kitchen to make a pot of tea.

The housekeeper stopped dusting and humming and looked up with a smile. "*Buongiorno, signorina!* Please, enjoy the *cornetto* with jam," she said, motioning to the counter.

"Thank you, I will."

She sat at the bar and ate a pastry topped with a sweet berry jam accompanied by an invigorating cup of morning tea sweetened with honey. This was the type of casual breakfast that she'd never been allowed to enjoy in the manor she'd grown up in.

Eating with the help was unheard of by both her parents. Forbidden, a lesson she learned late.

The few times she'd been caught in the kitchen chatting with the help, they had both been punished. She shifted, frowning as she tried to remember faces of servants that suddenly no longer worked for them. And then there were the more painful remembrances of workers who ceased treating her with familiarity.

Sitting here now while a housekeeper she didn't even know hummed and worked and chatted with her was a refreshing change. It was like living in a real home.

"These are delicious. Where did you buy them?"

The older woman laughed. "I make. It was my nonna's recipe, handed down from her mother." The woman waved a hand as if it progressed even further back.

"How lucky," Delanie said and meant it, earning her another smile.

She had absolutely no talents handed down from generation to generation. Or at least none that she would carry on.

"Have you lived in Montiforte long?" she asked the housekeeper.

"All my life," the woman said, returning to her work as if it were perfectly natural to do so among tenants. "My family has worked in the Toligara vineyards for generations." She frowned. "Signore Vincienta's grandfather was a good man who died too young. If he had been alive, the Toligara lands would never have been stolen. It was a bad three years in the valley working for the Englishman."

Delanie's face burned, not needing to know the man's name. She knew. Just like she knew how badly things had been under her father's care.

"It must have been a dreadful time," she said.

The housekeeper bobbed her head. "All is good again now that Signore Vincienta is managing Toligara."

Marco, of course. Interesting that such a stern man was so well loved by the people. That the business didn't bear his own arrogant name. But perhaps he was a better steward of the land and his employees than lover?

She pushed that arousing thought from her mind, but not before a giddy tightening streaked inside her. "Does your husband work in the Toligara vineyards?"

"No, the olive groves," she said. "I clean signore's house once a week."

"Really?"

Delanie strolled to the double doors and looked over the inviting terrace to the rolling hills beyond. Why would a billionaire only keep a weekly housekeeper when he could certainly afford fulltime staff? But then she recalled he maintained a minimal staff at Cabriotini Villa as well. Penury? Or was there another reason he shunned being waited on?

She shook her head, annoyed her thoughts were continually turned to Marco. But then it was clear he had a fan in his housekeeper, Delanie thought sourly.

"Is there a taxi service in Montiforte?" she asked.

The housekeeper laughed. "Montiforte isn't large enough for that."

"I had hoped to hire one to take me to the village."

"Why?" the housekeeper asked. "It is a short walk down the hill before you are on the upper alleyway of Montiforte."

"Oh. I hadn't realized it was that close," she said. The drive up had certainly seemed endless. But then time seemed to crawl when she was alone with Marco.

"I will clean your bedroom and en suite now, okay?" the housekeeper said.

"Yes, of course." She waved the woman on. "Do you have another house to clean today?"

"Oh, no. Signore pays me enough that I can work here one day a week."

The housekeeper disappeared into the bedroom, humming the same lilting tune she had earlier.

Delanie took three steps after the woman then stopped dead. No, she had to have misunderstood the housekeeper. This couldn't be Marco's house.

But as she turned in a slow circle, taking in the details she'd overlooked last night, it was clear this wasn't a rental. This was a home, with a few framed photos on the fireplace mantel and other personal touches strewn around.

But a billionaire's home?

No, it couldn't be. This quaint farmhouse nestled in the hills couldn't be where Marco lived.

Still, to be sure, she marched into the front bedroom and flung open the closet door. His spicy scent enveloped her as a dizzying surge of awareness spiraled up her limbs.

As if that weren't proof enough, suits, trousers, shirts hung in precise order. All were clearly high-end garments. All were his size.

She spun around, face flaming as her gaze flicked over the huge bed freshly made. The dresser with a minimum of clutter atop it. The jacket he'd worn yesterday was tossed haphazardly on a chair.

Her fingers tightened on the doorknob. Her blood cooled, glazed over with ice.

Damn him! He'd brought her to his home and had had the audacity to spend the night in the room next to her.

Fine! One night spent in his company didn't qualify. But she certainly wouldn't spend another with him in the next room, not when he'd made it clear that he desired her. Not when her body was at odds with her convictions, readily melting at his slightest provocation.

"Do you know where I might find a bed and breakfast or inn close by?" Delanie asked, standing in the bedroom she'd used last night and realizing the paintings on the wall were authentic.

Wealth. It had been all around her yet she'd failed to recognize it.

"You are leaving?" the housekeeper asked.

Delanie smiled. "It would be more practical if I stay right in town."

The housekeeper shook her head and returned to dusting. "There are two in the village but you won't find a room. The wine festival begins in a few days."

Montiforte would certainly be teeming with people and would have the best of the region on display. That could make planning the wedding far easier.

But to stay in the villa with Marco? To be secluded here?

An ache streaked across her midsection again and tightened. Desire. It had been so long since she'd felt it this keenly. Ten years to be exact.

No, she couldn't do this. Couldn't be close to him again.

"How far away is the nearest village?" she asked the housekeeper as she burst into the sunbathed kitchen.

Silence answered her. The room was empty.

A quick check of the salon confirmed she was the only one here. Her shoulders slumped. The housekeeper had left.

The housekeeper who came weekly to Marco's house.

She jabbed her fists at her sides. How could she have been so blind? How had she not known he was sleeping in the room next to hers?

CHAPTER SIX

DELANIE grabbed her bag which held all she would need for planning and breezed out onto the terrace.

Walking was invigorating. Walking just might clear her head of those unbidden, unwanted thoughts that kept intruding about Marco.

And even if it didn't, she needed to go to Montiforte and make sure there wasn't a room to be had.

The heels on her sandals clicked on the terra-cotta tiles that spanned the terrace. She frowned, wishing she had a more substantial shoe for the walk but the only other footwear she had with her were black pumps.

So personal shopping was high on her agenda as well.

As she reached the edge of the patio, the grandeur of the area literally took her breath away and pushed all other worries to the back of her mind. This was heady stuff for a girl raised in the city.

She shielded her eyes and stood as close to the edge as she dared. For as far as she could see, the beauty never ended.

Autumn painted the undulating countryside in a patchwork blanket of varying greens and golds. Interspersed among the hills were villages, clusters of buildings stacked into the hillsides.

In the distance she glimpsed a river winding through the valley, its details muted by distance into a wash of greens and blues, like a Monet painting come to life. On the rolling hills stretched neat rows upon rows of vines, all laden with plump grapes so dark a blue they gleamed nearly black in the sunlight.

She breathed in the fresh air as she stood where the hill dropped off into a gentle slope, the trail leading downward to nothing more than a graveled meandering path wide enough for two. The day was beautiful and calming, the sun warm on her face and arms with the breeze just cool enough to make the exertion of a walk pleasurable.

In moments she slipped under the charming Roman arch crusted with lichen and onto a narrow path that wound down the hill. Gray stone crunched underfoot and the trill of song-birds sang to her from high in the trees. The tiered gardens built into the hillside still overflowed with small orange and yellow blossoms, their color emphasized by gold and rust leaves.

But despite the allure on the terraced hillside and the spine of mountains looming in the distance, Marco remained in her thoughts. He had always been a fever in her blood and now was no different. In fact, now might be worse.

One touch, one taste only left her wanting more. Even though she knew it was folly, knew she would be the one hurt in the end, she couldn't banish the dreams of lying in his arms just once more.

Clearly she was mad. What else could explain why she was attracted to the man who'd hurt her?

She shook her head and moved on, focusing on the curved stone archway of a building that protruded from the hillside, its side covered in vines. A truck was parked nearby, its bed heaped with harvested grapes.

Her gaze fixed on the man striding toward her, broad shoulders squared and face drawn in a scowl that was darker than midnight. Marco, she realized, even before she got a clear look at his face.

He wore jeans so faded they were nearly white and a black

sweater that molded to his muscular chest and hugged his lean hips. His attire was so casual and so worn he could have passed for the lorry driver.

Her skin pebbled as fluttery ribbons of awareness wrapped around her, holding her tight to the spot. With effort she squared her shoulders and lifted her chin, determined to meet him head-on. To be practical and all business.

His hot gaze paused for a moment on the flimsy sandals dangling from one hand to her very bare feet. One brow lifted.

Her toes curled as did something low in her belly.

"Beautiful but impractical," he said.

She wasn't sure if he meant her in general or the straps of leather that she slipped on her tired feet. "I didn't have anything else but heels which would have been dangerous. If you would have just let me return home to pack—"

"Why are you here?"

Well, what did she expect? Pleasantries? A warm greeting?

"I am on my way to Montiforte," she said and managed a polite smile. "Why didn't you tell me the villa was yours?"

"There was no reason to." He glanced at his watch with a scowl. "I'll drive you to Montiforte."

"That's not necessary. Your housekeeper told me it was an easy walk," she said, the breathy catch in her voice mocking her stamina.

The last thing she wanted to do was be alone with him. If he hadn't kissed her, if her body hadn't so readily responded, she might be able to suffer through his company. But after having his hands on her, his lips devouring her own and setting her blood on fire, she couldn't risk it. He was simply too dangerously appealing and those memories she'd never been able to purge from her thoughts were rushing forward, tempting her with wild ideas of how good it could be with him.

"I insist. Come. Let me show you the winery and then we will have lunch," he said.

"Marco, I must get to town." Must get away from him while she could, while she still had the will to resist him.

"You can spare a half hour," he said. "There is a bistro in Montiforte that serves excellent fare. I insist you join me."

Of course he would. The cosmic force that was solely Marco engulfed her, threatened to wash her out into an uncharted sea that terrified her and enticed her.

"I appreciate the offer but I have a lot to do." Like visit the shops without Marco's company, without sharing lunch with him which sounded far too much like a date. "Time is short to get everything in order."

He waved her worry away. "As it is for me, overseeing the harvest as well as finalizing preparations for the festival. But we both must eat. As for wine, it goes without saying that we will serve our label at the wedding, but you should sample it so you are aware what foods would best be served."

What to say? She had every reason to trust in their contract that precisely detailed her duties and her reward for complying, but the fact that he'd lied about owning the villa kept her suspicions alive.

Her father had excelled at rescinding offers and finding loopholes in contracts. She had no idea if Marco had become just as ruthless.

"Point taken," she said. "The housekeeper mentioned the festival, but I hadn't realized it coincided with harvest and the wedding."

He threaded fingers through his thick hair. "Yes, too much happening at once. And not just here but throughout Umbria. It's maddening."

"And now a wedding," she said, and wished that his smile hadn't warmed her so. But it had and there was no denying her attraction to him.

"*Si*. This way." He laid a hand at the small of her back and urged her forward.

Her skin burned beneath his palm, the heat seeping into her

bones and leaving her weak-kneed. But she forced her legs to move, taking each step with care and hoping he didn't notice how much his touch affected her.

The interior of the winery was a welcome distraction, a beautifully vaulted space with warm terra-cotta floors and ancient-looking frescoed walls that simply took her breath away. "This is absolutely gorgeous."

"My great-great-grandfather built the winery and a local painter did the walls. Generations have added on to the structure but none have touched the fresco."

"Nor should they ever."

"Precisely. I made necessary repairs once I'd reclaimed it, but for the most part this building is as it had been four generations ago. Come, let me show you the rest." He slipped his arm around her shoulders and escorted her through the room, accompanied by the gawks of onlookers, as if it were the most natural thing to do, as if they hadn't been separated for ten years.

An electric shiver eddied through her, bringing every sensation awake. Her blood hummed from the contact, from the promise in his touch and from the memory of pleasure untold.

She hated that he still had this effect on her even though she savored this connection. The contradiction in her baffled her and she hated that as well. Hated that he could control the situation and her, hated that a part of her would always want this closeness.

He stepped from her and she just caught herself from grabbing him and holding on to this fragile contact. Her face burned at the admission. Thankfully he was busy moving something out of the walkway so he didn't notice her flush.

She tore her gaze from the man who commanded too much of her thoughts and gave her chilled arms a brisk rubbing. The room was stacked to the arched ceiling with oak barrels, and a pungent aroma hung in the air.

"You are cold." He grabbed a man's jacket off a peg and

swept it around her shoulders before she could protest wearing a communal garment.

His scent drifted off the fabric and she stilled, knowing this was his. Another puzzlement that was solely Marco.

She had never thought a man in his position would hang his coat among the workers' rough jackets. Yet common sense told her that he would need this if he spent any amount of time here and she knew he must. Knew that Marco wasn't just a man to spout orders or supervise—that he was one who would lend his back to a task as well.

And that only served to remind her that she really had never known Marco Vincienta at all.

"Thank you," she managed, clutching the jacket close and welcoming the warmth. "I didn't realize the winery was so large."

"It is deceiving from the outside. This is actually a natural cave that has been used by the Toligara family for centuries." He motioned above them to the network of round pipes. "I've made substantial changes to modernize the winery. These pipes carry the new wine to the casks."

"Why so many?"

"Each is a different type of wine, and they must not be mixed."

"Wow," she said, lowering her gaze to find him watching her with eyes that held an intimacy she didn't wish to explore here with her defenses already in tatters. "How badly did my father damage it?"

"The winery and olive groves suffered minimal damage. But the vineyards…" He paused and a shadow crossed his eyes. "There were few vines left alive and those needed much nurturing. Each day that I struggled to rebuild I hated your father more, not for his stealth in acquiring my family's business but for maliciously destroying it."

"You hated me just as much or more," she said.

He moved toward her with predatory grace, eyes locked

with hers. She tried to make her shaky legs move but they got the message late, managing to do no more than shuffle back a fraction, his advancing steps besting her retreating ones.

"I tried to but I could not," he said, the scratch in his usually controlled voice catching her by surprise. "What about you, *cara*? Do you hate me still?"

Her back slammed against the wall, the stones cool and hard against her spine, his gaze hot and probing hers. That familiar tingling danced over her heart, her belly, before settling low between her legs. She clenched her muscles, willing the needy sensations away, but that only made the ache more intense, more demanding.

The woodsy scent that was uniquely his enveloped her. He was far too close. Far too powerful. Far too tantalizing.

"I have no feelings toward you at all."

"Not even desire?" he asked.

"No, none," she said with surprising nonchalance.

His gaze drilled into her and she squirmed, her insides twisting and her heart hammered against her ribs. "You're lying, *cara*. The rapid pulse in your throat tells me your heart is racing. Your eyes are dilated with your need and your nipples are peaking through your shirt. If I put my hand between your legs would you be wet for me too?"

Damn him! Was she that transparent? "I'm here to do a job, Marco. Get that through your head. Nothing more."

He smiled but that left her more uneasy. "You do realize you cannot escape the inevitable," he said, a note of amusement ringing in his voice that echoed in the cavernous keeping room.

She was realizing far too much being alone with him. Feeling far too natural with him. It was bad enough her body betrayed her, weeping for his touch, throbbing for the press of his steely length against her.

But to think the past could have easily gone a different route terrified her.

"I don't know what you're talking about."

"Yes, you do," he said. "Us."

"There is no us," she said, her upthrust palms warning him to back off.

Marco filled her vision, filled her world. His gaze probed so deeply she shivered as his intimate touch whispered over her heart, her soul.

He planted both palms on the wall behind her, forcing her to draw her hands in to her breasts to keep from touching his oh-so-admirable chest. How easily he caged her in, towering over her, standing so close she could see the tiny flecks of gold light his dark eyes with a sensuous glow that made her body cry for him.

Marco was everything she had always wanted and everything she should avoid in a man.

That was never more evident than now. So why did her body refuse to listen?

"Yes, there is an us," he said, stroking his thumb along her jaw and smiling when she surrendered to a shiver. "There will always be us."

She shook her head and crushed her fists against her traitorous heart. Pride kept her from admitting he was right, and right now pride was all she had to cling to.

He pushed away and extended his hand to her, his gaze challenging. "Come. Our table is waiting."

"I've lost my appetite." Delanie smoothly ducked beneath his arm and strode toward the door, determined to walk the distance. To run if she must.

Marco allowed a small smile and enjoyed the enticing sway of her hips. "Where are you going?"

"To Montiforte."

"I'll drive you," he said, catching up with her easily before she'd made it halfway across the entryway.

"Thanks, but your housekeeper assured me it wasn't a long walk."

"I will take you."

That stopped her, as if his order had strings to pull her up short. She glanced back at him, body stiffened, not fully turning. But it gave him a clear view of the ripe fullness of her breasts pushing against her top.

A rosy flush kissed her neck and cheeks—from desire? Anger? Perhaps a bit of both over the way he bested her every attempt to avoid him.

The harder he pushed the more she pulled away, like magnets fighting an invisible force. But he wasn't about to back off.

He wanted her in his arms, in his bed where she belonged. At least for as long as she was here. Maybe this time when they parted he would be able to pluck her from his memory.

"Don't you have work to do?" Delanie asked.

"Nothing that can't wait," he said, exchanging a nod with his astute PA standing in the shadows who instantly disappeared to rearrange his schedule.

Her eyes, a clear blue that rivaled a Tuscan summer sky, met his and he found it difficult to draw a decent breath. The indecision reflected in her gaze clutched at his gut.

"Well, I do have things to do, mainly getting a wedding planned in short order," she said.

"You can begin after lunch," he said.

Her mouth thinned and for a moment he feared she would refuse. "Fine. We will eat and then I will get to work."

She resumed her rapid walk toward the door. He tarried a moment, enjoying the view of her firm bottom cupped in tight black denim.

Marco suffered the heaviness in his groin and strode after her. Outside he pressed his palm to the luscious small of her back and escorted her to his red Bugatti.

In moments he guided the sleek sports car down the hill toward Montiforte. "You won't find a room in the village."

"That's what your housekeeper told me."

"You don't believe her."

A beat of silence pinged between them. He could be a gentleman and remove himself from his house, giving her the privacy she sought—the distancing from him.

But he wanted her. Wanted? No he *had* to have her again. And he would have her, he vowed, allowing a smile.

Delanie looked through the window at the workers in the fields and heaved a sigh, her insides a jumble. "I know your housekeeper is probably right about the accommodations in Montiforte but I need to check."

"Then do, but know that even if you find a flat, you're better off staying at my villa."

"Better for whom?" she asked, shooting his arresting profile a glare. Why did he have to be so damned sexy?

His lips quirked in a half smile. "As I said earlier you are only prolonging the inevitable."

There it was again, that assurance that she would fall into his bed. Her faced heated, her breath quickening, her body so tightly wound with need she could scream. She couldn't ignore the pulse of need between her thighs any more than she could deny the emptiness in her arms. The longing for his lips on hers.

This was hell, and heaven would be found in his arms. But a romance with him would lead nowhere.

It couldn't, because she would not let herself slip under a man's control again. And yet she still wanted that carnal connection. Craved it. She still yearned for the crush of his powerful body on hers and the pinnacle of pleasure when he thrust into her, when passion took them to the beyond.

Sex. That was all Marco wanted from her. And—if anything—that was all she would allow herself with him, she swore on a shiver, knowing it would be glorious, fabulous sex.

"Your arrogance knows no bounds." She looked down at the hem of her top and cringed to find she'd wadded it in her fists. "Love was never part of the equation for you, was it?"

He snorted, his fingers tightening on the wheel, the muscle in his cheek ticking frantically. "Love. Woman do their damnedest to get men to give their hearts to them and men know that the fastest way to get a woman into bed is professing such devotion. I was not one of them. Ever."

"No. That was never a promise made and broken by you."

He sliced her a look so intense she felt her skin grow moist. "Are we back to doubting the other's word?"

"When did we ever fully trust the other?" she said.

His silence was answer enough.

He was her weakness. Her addiction. Her damnation? Time would tell on that one.

She had craved his love, wanted him, but had been too young at the time to realize that he wouldn't change. That love was an emotion he wouldn't or couldn't feel.

And still knowing all that she couldn't banish him from her thoughts. Couldn't stop comparing every man she met to Marco Vincienta and finding them all lacking.

She'd memorized every moment she'd been with Marco— the salty tang of his skin, the husk in his laugh, the electric golden gleam in his dark eyes when they were one, a heart-beat away from reaching nirvana.

Ten years was an awfully long drought to endure, even for a woman who'd only known one man. Too long.

"You're too quiet," he said. "Angry?"

She shook her head. "No. I'm resigned to the fact that you're a vital man and are used to getting what you want."

"Not always."

His right hand rested easy on the steering wheel, his control unmistakable, yet his big body was relaxed, almost as if he were one with the car, a powerful, pulsating thrust of energy that caught her up in his midst.

"That's hard to believe," she said.

"I didn't get you, *cara*," he said bluntly, and her thoughts ground to a jarring halt again.

"We were lovers."

He shrugged. "Briefly. I wanted more." He slid her a knowing look. "We were good together."

She'd thought so too. She'd spent endless nights dreaming of a future around this man.

"What we had is over," she said, needing to make that clear.

"Not necessarily."

He offered a cold proposition yet it stirred something hot inside her. Emotion and need shifted like tectonic plates in an angry sea, stirring up a tempest of sensual awareness that she hadn't felt in years.

This was what she'd blocked from her thoughts, tossed away like something to fear. This aching, gnawing sensation in the pit of her stomach told her something exciting was about to happen. That was the cause of the flush of heat and tingle of skin that swept over a woman when she was attracted to a man and was ready to act on that desire.

And she was attracted to Marco.

She would be lying if she said otherwise. The first instant she'd laid eyes on him she'd been lost, swept away to distant shores and silken sheets with just a caress, just a look. One kiss and she'd been lost.

He was her Prince Charming, her critical judge and the lover she carried in her heart. Now she had the chance to relive that glorious time with him one more time.

Dare she?

"It's over," she said, and hoped that it was so. "We're not the same people we were then."

"Perhaps that is for the best."

She chewed her lower lip, wishing she could be sure. There

was simply no way to know the type of man Marco had become in so short a time.

And where did that leave her?

The lush, hilly scenery passed by in a blur, the patchwork of olive groves and vineyards lost in a dark haze much like the picture she saw of her future. It had been so long since she'd allowed herself to dream big, to think in terms of just herself.

To be selfish.

Acting on her deepest desires now would be selfish. Dare she take what she wanted, even though she would likely leave Italy and him with a broken heart?

Too soon Marco zipped through an arched gatehouse flanked by a lane of rugged brick buildings. Green-, red- and maize-painted shutters hung at the tall windows, most open in midafternoon.

Clusters of potted plants sat by doorways and on crowded iron fire escapes that clung to the old buildings, their flowers sparse now. The brick-lined street narrowed and rose, slanting up against the buildings to the next level dominated by a piazza and fountain positioned right in the middle.

A moment later he wheeled the sports car under an arched portico covered with golden vines decorated with crimson leaves. He climbed out with fluid grace and opened her door, his hand firm and possessive as he helped her extract herself from the low-slung car.

Large white umbrellas shaded the street-side tables covered with white linens, the entire perimeter ringed with massive pots holding bushes, trees and a few flowers too stubborn to take their annual rest. "This doesn't look like a bistro to me."

"They have expanded the past year," he said, his hand at her back guiding her inside where a smiling maître d' greeted them.

"I have your table ready, Signore Vincienta," the man said. "Follow me."

She managed a glimpse of exquisite murals hanging on

exposed brick walls as they were led up a narrow flight of stairs to a private room. A cozy table for two sat before the tall windows, its linen cloth fluttering in the warm breeze.

Her stomach was doing much the same, thanks to Marco's hand still pressed to the small of her back. Their table was off in a nook, quite private. A perfect table for lovers, she thought as they took their seats.

He snapped his linen napkin open and flung it on his lap as the waiter appeared at his elbow. "Orvieto to start with antipasto," he told the waiter, but his gaze flicked to hers as he added, "It's a semisweet white, renowned in Umbria."

"That would be lovely," she said, fussing with her open napkin.

"*Tagliolini al tartufo bianco* for two," he told the waiter, his gaze still on hers.

She nodded her agreement for she really didn't care. It would be pure luck if she could manage a meal with her insides in such a twist.

He frowned, studying her closely. Her narrow shoulders were set in a tense line. Her smile looked strained. But she wasn't running, wasn't rebelling. *Patience,* he told himself.

"Relax," he said after he waved the maître d' on with a wine order.

If only she could...

She cleared her throat and took in the breathtaking vista of rolling hills beyond the aged walled village, but the thought that had taken root in her mind left her too giddy with nerves to appreciate its raw beauty. "I've given much thought about—us," she settled on, still hesitant to put a cold label on his proposition.

"Have you?" he asked, leaning back in his chair so he could admire her. "What have you decided?"

She met his gaze with the practised smile she'd used countless times in the course of entertaining her father's potential clients and affected her most cosmopolitan tone, hoping it would mask the riot of emotions running rampant inside her. "We're adults now. If we have an affair it must be discreet and brief, lasting no longer than my stay in Italy. It also must be safe for both of us."

The bold proposition had no sooner left her mouth than the waiter strode in and went straight to Marco, decanting a bottle of wine and pouring a suitable splash in his glass. His gaze narrowed on her for a taut moment but that was the only sign her words had had any effect on him and not necessarily a good one.

As was expected, he tasted the wine with a precision that had not been so defined years ago. A nod gave the waiter permission to pour and leave.

Marco leaned back in his chair, his wineglass cradled in one hand, his eyes locked on hers. Perspiration beaded her brow and dotted her bare shoulders.

"I agree. No strings. No surprises," he said at last, raising his glass. "A toast."

Face heated and body trembling with uncertainty, she dug deep for control and slipped her fingers around the heavy stem of her wineglass. She raised it and forced a calm smile that she certainly didn't feel.

"To?" she dared to ask, heart pounding and mouth desert dry.

He rocked forward, the movement as fluidly predatory as a jungle cat's. "To our affair."

With the clink of crystal and dueling of intense dark eyes with her own wide ones, her fate for a few weeks was sealed.

Marco drank, the bronzed column of his throat working, his gaze hot and fixed on hers. A flush stole over her skin, as intimate as a caress.

It was done. They would be lovers, and knowing Marco it would be soon. Perhaps even tonight.

She brought the glass to her lips with a hand that trembled, and took a drink, swallowing more than the ladylike sip she'd intended. A surge of heat swept over her as much from the alcohol as from the man and the need he stirred in her.

Already his essence was threading through her. And they had done no more than kiss once. She didn't want to guess how deeply embedded it would be after they made love.

"You still don't trust me," he said, and that brought her gaze snapping up to his again.

She didn't deny it. "That goes both ways."

He swirled his wine and smiled, a relaxed gesture that belied his power. "*Cara,* must I remind you that I have trusted you to arrange my sister's wedding?"

Good grief, but he was serious. "Yes, you trust me so much so you are living in the house with me, watching my every step."

His smile widened as he leaned forward, a glint in his eyes that stirred memories of them together, entwined. "I am living in the same house with you because I want you in my bed every night. Every free chance we have. There is no other reason."

The waiter bustled in with plates of food, his flurry of movement a welcome distraction for her to gain some semblance of calm. Not that she could with Marco staring at her with such intensity. Not that she could have formed a coherent sentence at that point.

Her body shook from the promise in his words, the hungry look in his eyes. It had come down to this, or maybe this had been his plan all along.

Force her here. Seduce her. Then walk out of her life again, this time forever.

She set her glass down and stared at her plate, knowing her nervous stomach wouldn't tolerate food. Still she sampled it, more to keep her hands busy and her gaze off Marco.

It was her choice. She could continue to fight her magnetic attraction to him and suffer a stressful, miserable stay in Italy or surrender to this raging desire and spend the next two weeks in his arms.

Either way her heart would break when they said their final good-byes and she returned to London, but by becoming his lover again there would be no regret. She would have had one last sizzling fling with Marco.

Besides this wasn't some stranger who failed to stir her interest or desire. This was Marco, the man she knew intimately. The man she loved.

Love. It had no place here, not in an affair. She could expect nothing from this but pleasure. The final closing of this chapter in her life when his sister's wedding was over and she returned to London alone.

"You are eating less than a bird," he said, having consumed a good portion of his meal.

"Sorry. I'm not hungry for food."

There was only one thing that would ease the tight coil pulsing in her belly. Sex.

She took a sip of wine and ran her tongue over her lips, all the while holding his gaze with hers, hoping he wouldn't laugh at her attempt at seduction.

The potent promise swirling in his eyes was more intoxicating than the wine, both leaving her head spinning, both sending heat coursing through her. But only he had the power to turn her into this soft wanton, breasts heavy and nipples tightening into hard buds.

Only Marco could make her hunger for sex. That's how she had to look at it. Anything else would simply crush her.

Marco took a drink of the rich wine, letting time drag out, watching as a bead of sweat dared to trickle down her slender neck. Nerves. She was a jumble of them. An act? Another contradiction that was solely Delanie?

"That is an innuendo that begs careful consideration," he said.

"If you feel that is necessary," she said, making some flippant wave of her hand.

"You don't?"

"Why wait when our time together is brief?"

Her voice had gone soft with a husk that left his blood pulsating with raw need. Years before they'd come together in a cataclysmic explosion of desire, wanted only the moment, wanted only what pleased them at the time.

Now they were adults, capable of setting barriers as well as tearing them down. That's just what she'd done, torn down the last fence separating them.

Sex between them wouldn't be new. They knew what to expect going into it, knew it wouldn't last. Knew that despite good intentions, somebody could walk away from it hurt.

"Let's get out of here," he said.

She nodded, her gaze lowered, her fingers fidgeting as she dropped her linen napkin on the table. "Yes, please."

For the second time, he noted that quiet reserve which was at odds with her agreement that they embark on an affair. But he wasn't going to dwell on that or on her sudden jitters. Or on the fact he was approaching sex with her as he would a mistress.

She deserved better than that. *They* deserved more as individuals and as a couple.

And he would see that she was treated like a queen—in his arms and out of them for the duration of her stay.

He rose silently and helped her to her feet, absorbing the tremor that shot through her when he grasped her elbow. That first teetering step she took, nearly wrenching free from him, demanded he tighten his hold on her.

"Sorry," she said, swaying slightly before gaining her balance on the same low sandals she'd worn walking down the hillside to the winery. "I'm okay now."

He wasn't convinced. "How much wine did you drink?"

She sent him a helpless look that caught him by surprise,

like a punch to the gut driving the air from his lungs. As though she trusted him.

"I'm not sure," she said, delicate brow puckered. "Every time I looked my glass was full."

His lips thinned, more annoyed at himself for not paying attention to the overzealous waiter. If he had, he certainly would have cautioned her for imbibing a bit more than necessary.

He slipped her hand through the crook in his arm, holding it there a moment when she jolted.

"Thank you," she said, relaxing but refusing to meet his gaze.

"My pleasure."

And it was, he admitted.

He heaved a sigh and got them out of the restaurant without much notice other than from the curious onlookers who recognized that Montiforte's most eligible bachelor was with a beautiful woman. Once in the car, he whipped through the streets toward the highway that would take them into the foothills.

"How do you feel?" he asked, flicking her a quick glance to find her curled a bit on her seat, head nestled against the leather back and dreamy eyes fixed on his.

She smiled, and a jolt of heat shot to his groin. "Very relaxed now. And you?"

"Fine," he gruffed out, shifting slightly to ease his growing torment.

But she wasn't looking at him. She was looking at the shadows creeping down the mountains into the valley.

"We will be there soon." Closer now that he was on the winding road that wound up from town.

"That's good."

He reached over and grasped her hand in his, something he'd done years ago with her. Something he'd only done with this woman. Her fingers twined with his, small and silken and lost in his big grip.

"I've missed this," she said, voice drowsy, fingers tightening on his.

He gave her hand a squeeze and something—emotion?—did the same to his heart. "So have I."

The evening was turning out to be warm, with a balmy breeze. The woman beside him was hot, willing. Relaxed.

He maneuvered the wheel with one-handed precision, his blood running as hotly as the high-powered engine slicing through the night.

Five more minutes and then he zipped down the poplar-lined drive to his villa.

"We're here," he said, killing the engine.

The silence was deafening, but the brilliant smile from a full moon shone down on them, showing Delanie with eyes closed, fast asleep.

He pressed back in his seat, his annoyance vanishing as he drank in her beauty. A smile tugged at his mouth. It was all he could do to contain his laughter at the irony of her capitulation and overindulgence.

Tonight would not be the night. But soon, he thought as he slipped from the car. As he gathered her in his arms and strode into the house, making straightway for the master bedroom.

Soon.

CHAPTER SEVEN

DELANIE stirred, opening her eyes a mere slit and saw nothing familiar. Sunlight flooded the room and she winced, snapping her eyes shut and pulling the bedsheet over her head with a groan.

Snippets of last night pinged through her memory. Too much fine wine. Too bold a decision. A long, seductive drive to the villa with Marco controlling the moment and her.

Another groan whispered from her as she pressed her face into the soft down pillow, forcing herself to relax, to let the tension seep from her. But that was denied her as a spicy scent filled her senses. Familiar. Seductive. Masculine.

Marco, of course.

She levered up on her elbows, staring at the place beside her, knowing his scent wouldn't be that strong unless he'd spent substantial time in this bed, holding her in his arms. The slightest indent visible in the pillow proved he'd been here.

That spicy scent that was uniquely his, that she'd never been able to forget, was all around her. On her bare skin.

Her breath came fast as she scrambled for the sheet, her gaze flitting around the large bedroom. Marco's, she recognized now.

Sunlight flooded through the windows to stream across the polished wood floor and wash over the clean modern lines of the furnishings. Her jeans and jersey were draped over a chair back. Her sandals lay willy-nilly on the floor.

She swallowed hard and slowly stretched, her skin chilling as she did a quick mental inspection of herself. He'd stripped her to her skin, not the first time but the first time she had no memory of it.

But they hadn't been intimate. She was sure of it.

If they had, her body would be replete with pleasure instead of humming with the same tension. She wouldn't be this tight physically or emotionally.

"Buongiorno," he said, striding into the room bearing a tray, his muscular body as bare and bronzed as his feet.

She damned the telling shiver that rippled through her in one long delicious wave, knowing full well they'd slept in each other's arms, skin against skin. "Good morning."

He set the tray down on the bed with a wink and climbed in beside her as if it were the most natural thing in the world. And at one time it had been.

But that thought came and went like lightning as she tried not to look at the naked man beside her. The strong, lean body she'd admired ten years ago had developed into sculpted slabs of muscle befitting a Roman God. Bronzed. Beautiful.

"I have fruit, brie and croissants." He popped a grape in his mouth and held another out to her. "It isn't much."

"It's fine. Lovely, actually," she said, taking a deep blue grape from his outstretched palm, rattled by his buff body and good mood in the face of her humiliating performance last night. "I'm sorry about drinking so much."

He shrugged one well-hewn shoulder and chewed, the frown pulling at his brow there and gone. "These things happen. You were tired and the waiter was being generous. We have tonight to look forward to."

She swallowed, shifting and nearly groaning at the throb between her legs that begged for release, a need that had erupted the second he'd walked into the bedroom and stretched out beside her.

"Yes, of course. I expected you would want to get reacquainted this morning," she said, damning the heat that burned her neck and cheeks, a red flag of embarrassment that warred with the carnal flush burning her pale skin.

He leaned so close she could see her obvious lust reflected in his eyes. Her cheeks burned even more, and the need inside her was so unbearable she thrashed her legs, hoping he would notice, praying he would touch her there and relieve the ache.

"As much as I would enjoy making love with you long into the morning, now is not the time," he said, trailing a finger down her neck, the upper curve of her breast and circling a nipple that grew hard and aching at his touch, that had her leaning into him. "I want to savor every second adoring you and I refuse to be rushed."

In the quiet wake of her bold capitulation and her ensuing inelegant behavior at the restaurant, the last thing she wished to do was show how malleable she was in his hands. Yet here she was, breath hitching, her breasts full and her very core crying with need for him.

"I want that too," she said, digging deep to find the strength to tear herself away from him, to sweep her shredded dignity around her like a sturdy wrap.

But she couldn't pull her gaze from his, couldn't scramble away when he leaned in, his big hands gliding up her bare arms, dredging a shiver from her that had nothing to do with the chill air and everything to do with the hot hard man.

His warm inviting breath on her face had her lifting her face to his in greedy invitation. She'd waited for this for so long. So long…

Her lips parted, heart hammering beneath her breasts. His mouth met hers with a groan, a soft brush of lips that fizzed in her blood like the finest champagne, sweet and intoxicating and going straight to her head.

"Marco," she breathed against his lips, her fingers splayed over his bare chest, the muscles hard, the skin hot and smooth, the sprinkling of dark hair crisp and slightly damp beneath her palm as she slid a finger down the chiseled contours of his body to his length thrusting hard against her thigh.

He sucked in a breath, pressing himself against her palm. The same insistent pulse she felt in him thrummed between her legs and deeper into her core where she ached for him to be. In her, part of her.

"Tonight," he said, grasping her hand and pulling it away.

His breath sawed hot against her neck, sending delicious chills rippling over her skin. It had been too long since she'd felt this wicked, this easy with a man.

He dropped one last lingering kiss on her too-sensitive skin, then sauntered away, his bare buttocks tight, his legs long and muscled. She clutched the sheet in both hands, the soft fabric abrasive to her sensitized nipples, trying to focus, trying to shake off the sensual haze swirling around her like early-morning fog.

She clenched her thighs together and stifled a groan, wanting him so badly she physically ached. Don't gawk at him. But she couldn't tear her eyes away from such masculine beauty. Couldn't forget how that strong body had felt on her, in her.

Modesty would goad most people to dress in private but Marco clearly didn't possess such inhibitions. He unabashedly stood in the opening of the dressing room and thrust long legs into navy trousers before shrugging into a pale blue shirt.

And she sat on the bed transfixed, drinking in every second. Branding it all on her memory.

His mobile trilled no more than twice before he answered and moved into the shadows. He was too far from her and his voice was pitched too low to understand a word, but the sudden tensing of his broad shoulders alerted her that the news wasn't good.

"I should return before dark," he told her, striding from the dressing room without glancing her way.

And just like that the playboy she'd dined with last night and had a teasing respite with this morning was gone, hidden behind a custom-made suit that was undoubtedly Italian and clearly tailored to fit his admirable physique.

"I have a lot to do as well," she said—starting with a trip to a women's clothing shop.

"*Si,* the wedding," he said, pausing at the door. "A selection of clothes and shoes will be delivered for you today."

Just what a rich man would do for his mistress. That tainted what they'd agreed on. Brought it down to a level that made her skin crawl. Yet wasn't that what she had agreed to? A brief affair? To be his mistress for two weeks?

She seized a quick breath, chin held high, as the bubble of euphoria inside popped to rain ice on her blood. "Thanks, but I prefer choosing my own clothes."

"I prefer buying these gifts for you," he drawled. "But if you wish, consider them as compensation for dragging you from London with the clothes on your back."

"Fine. Thanks." She would purchase her own clothes and when she left she'd take them and leave his behind.

His brow furrowed as he executed a perfect knot in an indigo silk tie and snugged it to his throat with a quick twist of his wrist. "Just so you know, I have never brought a woman here before."

What was she supposed to say to that? *You're kidding... Thank you...*

In the end she said nothing because her libido was shorting out her brain cells with the way his gaze was fixed on her, peeling away the sheet she clutched to her bosom, kissing skin that was moist and flushed with desire.

How could he make her nearly come with a look?

The control she'd had the past ten years was nonexistent now in the face of his potent sensuality. Which made this entire job all the more challenging to endure.

But she would get through. She wanted to get through it!

She had to do a stellar job, had to garner the top publicity this wedding would offer her. Had to have this last fling with Marco because…

Because she wanted him.

She'd willingly added an affair to her list of things to accomplish here because of that burning desire. Selfish and carnal and so unlike her, but that was the truth.

Her only saving grace was the ability to hide the emotions rioting in her, a knack perfected as she'd suffered the company of businessmen eager to align with Tate Unlimited. Men who'd thought the fast track to getting to the top of Tate Unlimited was to woo her. But she'd kept them all at arm's length, earning the reputation of being an ice princess. All but Marco.

"Give me a ring if you need me," he said.

"I shall," she said, managing a smile.

He stared at her a long assessing moment before striding from the house. But she didn't draw a decent breath until she heard the powerful roar of the Bugatti racing away.

Dusk cast a surreal glow over the vineyards stretching to the foothills and had turned the tiled roofs of Montiforte a fiery red by the time Marco returned from Rome. It had been a stressful day and he was eager to conclude it and return to Delanie.

But that would have to wait, thanks to a problem at the Toligara press. The man who always oversaw issues like this was off to Arezzo for the night with his wife of thirty-five years, celebrating their anniversary.

Though Marco hated postponing his evening with Delanie, he wasn't about to ruin a trusted employee's happy occasion. Besides, his time with Delanie should be savored like fine wine, savored to its fullest.

In bed and out of it.

He tugged his phone from his pocket and punched in her number, one that he'd put in over a month ago but had never called. "Are you through for the day?" he asked when Delanie answered with a hesitant greeting.

"Almost. I am finalizing the date for a fitting and should be back to the house in thirty minutes or so," she said. "Are you there?"

Was that a note of dread in her voice?

"No, I have just reached Montiforte," he said. "There was a problem at the oil press that needs my attention. I've no idea when I'll return home."

"Oh, I'm sorry to hear that."

"That is good to know," he said, smiling. "How did your day go?"

"Productive. I've arranged for Bella's first fitting with the dressmaker tomorrow and should have sample arrangements of flowers ready for her approval by then as well. Tomorrow I'll see that all is in readiness for the church, then I'll tour the castle where she wishes to hold the reception."

As her contract dictated, she told him about the businesses she'd contacted, her preferences for each and why she'd chosen to work with locals.

"I was amazed at what was available here and their willingness to adapt. It's a good start," she said.

He smiled, hearing the enthusiasm in her voice. "It seems you have everything in line."

"There is still much to do," she said. "Bella expressly stated she did not want the men in tuxedos so I spoke with the tailor. But she's also decided she wants a blend of traditional and modern so I'll arrange a very relaxed Mediterranean theme."

"I doubt the groom will complain about the lack of formality," he said, and neither would he.

"Just what I thought as well," she said. "There are two photographers of note in Montiforte and both of their works are good. But I'd prefer gathering samples to show Bella since each one has a far different style."

"My sister is quick to speak her opinion," he said.

She laughed. "That is obviously a family trait."

He laughed, enjoying this banter. Enjoying her.

"True. I want you, *cara.* How is that for expressing my opinion?"

He heard her breathing, quick and hurried. "To the point. Honest, and I appreciate honesty."

"As do I," he said, serious again.

"Good, because I want this as well," she said in a whisper that hummed through his blood.

A new tension surged between them in waves. Hot and intense. A tension that had nothing to do with his sister's wedding and everything to do with their affair.

"I regret this postponement," he said.

"There is always tomorrow."

Every nerve in his body screamed for release tonight. Now. His biological father would have let the workers deal with the mess at the mill and gone off to meet the lady.

Which is exactly what he would not do, he vowed as he neared the olive press. This was his company. His problem to solve.

Ah, but if he just had a few more minutes to at least talk with Delanie…

"Have a good evening, *cara,*" he said as he killed the engine.

"Yes, you as well."

"Delanie," he said, rolling her name over his tongue, savoring it as he had hoped to do to her tonight.

"Yes."

"Tomorrow will be our time," he said. "We'll start with dinner."

And end up in bed.

She didn't reply, but then no words were necessary. Tomorrow he would have her in his arms where she belonged.

* * *

As busy as she'd been all day, she should have fallen into an exhausted sleep. But here it was near two in the morning and she was still wide awake.

Delanie hugged her arms to her bosom and strolled back to the glass doors that opened onto the terrace. A bloated moon bathed the hills in a wash of silver, the effect almost magical.

It was a vista one wouldn't easily tire of, she thought.

The hum of an engine broke the stillness a heartbeat before headlamps cut through the night. Marco's Bugatti, winding back up the hill. She recognized the deep purr of the powerful engine.

Even if she hadn't, some sense told her that Marco was returning home. The velvety hush of the night drifted around her, as darkly sensual as the man behind the wheel.

She chafed her bare arms, trembling like a leaf caught in the wind, burning inside with an emotion she hadn't felt in years. An emotion she never wished to feel again for Marco Vincienta.

Yet it was there. Intense. Demanding.

A true mistress would greet him at the door with open arms. She would be wearing one of the sexy outfits he'd had delivered today, clothes she had no intention of wearing.

His mistress would lead him to the bedroom and satisfy the ache throbbing between them. But that wasn't her.

The car rounded the curve, the headlights sweeping across the front of the villa. She bit her lip and stepped back into the shadows, shaking, knowing she couldn't do it.

It took but a moment to return to her room. Another to close the door silently as the metallic click of his car door echoed in the night.

She crawled into bed and lay stiff as a board, waiting. Trying to listen to his footsteps over the pounding of her heart.

Come to me, she silently willed him.

The front door opened and closed. Steady steps made their

way across the living room. Another door opened and closed. Close, but not hers.

She bit her lip again, restless. It wasn't too late. She could go to him still.

Who was she kidding?

He'd rebuffed her the first time she'd flirted with him ten years ago, choosing his own moment to catch her alone with her defenses down. He'd rejected her the night he'd left her and England.

No, she simply couldn't make the first move again. Not tonight. Maybe never.

Marco stepped onto the terrace the following morning, muscles snapping taut as he watched Delanie stroll along the perimeter of an olive grove, her mobile pressed to her ear. A light breeze sent her long hair rippling down her back in a golden waterfall of silk. The full sun kissed her bare arms and legs with a honey-gold light.

Tonight she would be his. Tonight he would know if that curtain of hair felt as silken draping his arms, his chest, his groin. He would know if her smooth skin tasted as sweet as pomegranates on his tongue.

Dammit, he'd spent a miserable night staring at the ceiling, fighting the urge to go to her. As badly as he wanted her, he knew a coupling then would be less than satisfying.

His fingers tightened around the cup of coffee he held, his chest pillowing out as he inhaled heavily. Nothing had changed. She was the only woman he had ever burned this intensely for, still ached to kiss, hold, drive into her with all the passion simmering in his soul.

She was the one he'd come to care about. The one who'd roused a fury in him he hadn't known he possessed.

His gut pinched. A jolt scraped over his nerves and lifted the hair at his nape.

The anger resulting from Delanie's lies was a fool's emotion yet he couldn't deny its existence any more than he could deny his desire for her. The fact it plagued him now confirmed he'd yet to trust her fully.

Trust. Such a simple word. Such a difficult thing to achieve with another person. Impossible with Delanie.

He sipped his coffee. Huffed another terse sigh and welcomed the flood of sanity that washed to sea those darker, selfish thoughts.

Delanie Tate was here on business. And he had every right to stand here and watch her, to drink in her beauty and poise until he was sated.

And so he did.

Her stride was sure yet unhurried. But there was something about her posture that screamed tension. The slight bowing of her shoulders. The lowered head. The free hand that splayed and fisted before the call obviously ended and she just stood there, staring at her mobile.

His brow furrowed. Something was wrong. Personally? The wedding?

It was the last that prompted him to make a quick call to his PA to clear his schedule for the day and night. He had no idea of her plans, but whatever they were he had no intention of letting Delanie do it alone.

If there was a problem brewing he would do all he could to help her. He would go with her as silent support. To smooth the way for stubborn merchants. To be with her, watching her at work in her world.

When her day was finished, they would celebrate with a bit of *vino* and a lot of *amore.*

He smiled. That couldn't come soon enough.

This driving desire would ease the more they were together. When she left him this time, he would be ready to see her go.

And if he was wrong...

He set his empty cup down and stormed down the steps,

refusing to consider that this plan could backfire on him, that he could end up burned again by the same woman.

She stopped on the edge of the flagstones, her gaze widening on his across the expanse, looking a bit windblown and sexy as hell. Looking flustered as well.

A silky blue blouse draped over full breasts and peaked over nipples that he longed to caress, kiss, draw deeply into his mouth. Her simple tan skirt hugged her hips to a point just above her knees, exposing a good length of strong creamy legs.

New clothes. Items he wouldn't have chosen, yet on her they were alluring.

"At work already?" he asked.

"Yes, your sister rang moments after I stepped out here," she said, a telling frown marring her smooth brow. "Bella refuses to consider either local photographer, insisting I hire someone who can capture what she feels."

He swore, certain his sister was being temperamental just for the pleasure of it. Just because she could.

"She is being unreasonably difficult," he said. "She is beautiful. In love. With child. That won't change no matter who takes the pictures."

"No, it does matter. If she's uncomfortable it will show in her pictures," she said. "She wants me to visit a photographer in Florence. A childhood friend that she's hesitant to contact herself."

"Why?"

"I gathered their last parting was painful and not mutual and she fears he will refuse her," she said. "But Bella wants him to take the shots for her wedding, reception and some honeymoon pictures."

"What was he to her?"

"I don't know." She sighed. "I thought I could find that out when I phoned him, but he demands to talk face to face with the bride and groom or the wedding planner before accepting the job. Bella wants me to appeal to him, so I need to travel there today. Depending on how well things go I may not return until quite late tonight or early tomorrow."

He scrubbed a hand over his mouth, believing her. This is what she was reputed to do best—ensure that the bride was pleased. But to let her visit this photographer alone? Spend a night in Florence? Unacceptable!

"Fine. We leave whenever you are ready."

Her lips parted and the pulse point in her throat thrummed wildly. "We?"

His smile widened, tempted to lave and kiss that warbling pulse until she moaned. "I assure you I won't be in your way."

Her gaze narrowed and he braced himself, expecting her to argue. But it would do her no good. He wasn't about to let her out of his sight for long.

As if reading his mind, she squared her slumping shoulders. "I am equally sure you will be, but given the circumstances I have little choice. Give me a moment to gather my things."

He smiled, ready to give her all the time she needed.

Delanie hurried into her room and hoped her haste gave the impression of diligence instead of escape. Mercy, how would she get through a day and possibly a night in sunny, sensual Florence with Marco at her elbow?

Her senses were too raw around him, her desire for him growing stronger by the day. Why had she agreed to be his mistress for the duration? Where was her backbone?

She pinched her eyes shut, hating the hollow ache in her heart that confirmed she was vulnerable to him. A future with Marco was out of the question.

Though he refused to acknowledge any similarity to her father, she saw the parallels. Marco dominated everything in his life, his world. Those tendencies could take an ugly turn and she could end up tied to a man like her father.

She wouldn't repeat her mother's mistakes and suffer in silence, chained by love.

Now more than ever she needed to prove to herself they were only good together for the short term, that she hadn't made a horrid mistake ten years ago. That she wasn't making one now.

When she left him and Italy, it would be with the assurance that she'd been right. They made great lovers. That was all.

She would return to England and tuck her memories of Marco into a secret place in her heart. Move on with her life.

Closure, at last, would be hers.

And if she was wrong?

An hour later she was in Florence, having worked on last-minute plans on her electronic notepad while Marco drove and spoke with his PA via his mobile. But it was still a struggle for her to keep her mind on her work with him sitting beside her, effortlessly commanding the Bugatti as they whizzed up the winding *autostrada* with the Apennines rising to her right while lush vineyards and olive groves and a meandering river stretched as far as the eye could see.

The fertile landscape and fresh air were a feast. The man beside her remained the decadent dessert she hungered to savor.

When she'd first met him so long ago, she'd fallen as much in lust with him as love. Perhaps more so.

Now she was seeing the man he'd become. Powerful. Ruthless. More fascinating than any man she'd ever met.

She still desired him, not with that wild hungry craving of youth. But with a woman's appreciation of his strong, honed body and keen mind.

It would be so easy to fall back into an intimate relationship with him. So tempting to lose herself just once more in his arms. So easy to convince herself that an affair could develop into something lasting.

It was an illusion she must definitely guard against.

He already held her business in his grip. She dared not let him claim her heart again as well.

But how could she stop the inevitable?

She cast his beautifully sculpted profile a surreptitious look. Desire ribboned around her but it was the warmth stealing around her heart that confirmed she was already doomed.

"You've been terribly quiet," Marco said, feeling her gaze stroking over him yet again.

His blood raced, sending a surge of heat to his already uncomfortable groin. This woman was torturing him just by being near. And he had the entire day to spend with her in Florence!

"The photographer has samples on his website and I took the opportunity to study them and make a few notes," she said, slipping her slim notepad back into her oversize bag.

"I trust you're impressed with his work."

"He's very talented."

What she hadn't said raised his curiosity. "He is someone you would hire then."

Her brow creased, fueling his misgivings. "I'll know more once I've met with him."

"If you feel he's not right, we can turn around now."

"And disappoint Bella? No way." She inhaled sharply, her chin coming up in that bulldog determined way of hers that he admired and disliked in equal measure. "I intend to make this appointment and judge his talents for myself."

He smiled, his fingers stroking the steering wheel as he crossed the River Arno, the deep blue water reminding him of Delanie's eyes when she climaxed. And wasn't that a hell of a thing to remember when he was already tight with lust for her?

"We should arrive at the photographer's studio shortly," he said, trying to think of anything but the woman beside him.

She stiffened, the sudden chill in the car making his skin bead. "I don't want you interfering in my business."

He held a palm toward her. "I am there as nothing more than your assistant."

"Are you crazy?" she asked. "Everyone in Italy must know who you are from the press."

He scowled, his teasing mood and desire freezing over instantly. "I have avoided the press since my rise and I intend it to stay that way. Trust me when I say I won't be telling a photographer who I am."

CHAPTER EIGHT

MARCO'S promise needled Delanie as he traversed the congested narrow streets of Florence with the skill of a Formula 1 driver. The gray stone mass of the ancient city with the occasional building painted yellow or green failed to draw her interest away from the colorful man behind the wheel.

It seemed inconceivable that someone who'd risen to such power and who'd inherited a millionaire's business could escape notoriety. But he'd done that, choosing to hide his identity behind a ghost corporation.

She could understand the need for anonymity in his business dealings. But why did he feel the same need to stand in the shadows in sunny Italy?

Moments later, he smoothly parked near the Signoria Square with its impressive Neptune's fountain that she'd read about in school. Though fabulous to see, the statue's generous physique paled beside Marco's.

She surrendered to a delicious shiver as the object of her delight and turmoil escorted her up a narrow passageway on rugged stone stairs that had climbed the sides of gray stone buildings for centuries. Though serviceable, they hadn't been made for dainty heels that seemed to find every little glitch and imperfection in the stone.

She stepped wrongly a heartbeat later and swayed, but Marco caught her up with a strong arm around her waist.

Her breath caught and every nerve in her body zinged as if shocked.

"These steps are wicked," she said, trying to extract herself from his steely hold.

"Perhaps I should carry you the rest of the way," he said, his breath warm and welcome on her face.

Too welcome.

She got her balance and eased from him. "Perhaps I should take off my shoes."

His lips pulled into a smile that sent her insides tumbling. "Isn't that how we met?"

"I—I don't remember." She slipped off her slings and hurried up the steps, leaving him and that memory behind her.

But not for long.

Marco was beside her an instant later and so was the sweet erotic memory of the first time they'd met. Holland Park, on what must have been the hottest day London had seen in decades.

That's where Marco found her. He'd followed her from her father's office and found her barefoot at the edge of the water that moved calmly around her ankles.

"I'm fairly certain going into the water is forbidden by the park officials," he'd drawled, his Italian accent lending his voice a very seductive tone that whispered over her bare arms and legs and left her tingling.

She'd whirled to confront him and was temporary struck dumb as she realized her intruder wasn't a park attendant or a constable but a very handsome, very virile stranger. "Most likely you're right."

"Want to talk about it?"

Nobody had ever asked her if she needed a shoulder to lean on or cry on. Her father issued orders. Her mother begged her for support.

But nobody ever asked Delanie Tate if she wanted to talk about what bothered her.

It was so unheard of, such a phenomenal event that she left the water's edge and crossed to the handsome stranger with a breathy, "Yes."

That day she'd fallen into Marco Vincienta's arms and his bed—another first for her. She shirked off her fears of trusting a man, turning to putty in Marco's capable hands as he whisked her away into passion she'd not known existed.

In less than a week she'd lost her heart to him. And she was terrified because she was swiftly becoming emotionally dependent on a man, just like her mother. Marco had been so dominating, so aloof, yet so passionate with her.

That fear that she would repeat her mother's hell had been the one thing that kept her on edge, that stopped her from fully trusting him, even though her body loved his touch, his kiss.

And that wounded look in his eyes had melted something in her. Left her wanting to hold him. Heal his hurts.

Now she saw how wrong she'd been. How she'd let fear cloud her vision. Marco was ruthless, able to mete out vengeance to those who deserved it. But he wasn't mean. Wasn't abusive. Wasn't vindictive.

Marco Vincienta was the direct opposite of her father. And she loved him still, maybe more than ever before.

Now he pressed his hand to the small of her back, hot and possessive. She gasped and whirled around, skin on fire.

Big mistake, she realized a heartbeat later. The cold rough stone wall was at her back, a massive pillar to her right, and filling the narrow void was Marco.

"You're lying, *cara mia,*" he said, hands bracketing her shoulders to hem her in, head bent close so only she heard him. "You remember those first days together when we gave and took equally, just like I remember them."

Her heart raced, her mind spun those memories of when she'd fallen in love with Marco to life. When their passion had terrified her. When she'd thought she could hold back from surrendering all to him and still hold on to the man.

She'd convinced herself Marco could do business with her father and keep their relationship separate. That beside him, she could continue to protect her mother. How very wrong she'd been.

Yes, she remembered the joy, the passion. A tingle raced up her spine as she focused on the beautifully masculine sculpt of his mouth. How she'd struggled the first time to hold a part of her from him. How she'd failed then.

Now she was stronger. Resisting him should be easy. But her knees quaked and her blood hummed the longer she stared into his eyes, reading the passion, the promise, the purpose. Was he going to kiss her? Out here on the street? Was she going to let him?

No, she couldn't let herself go again. She slammed both palms against his chest and shivered at the power and heat radiating from him into her. Moisture gathered under her breasts and between her thighs.

"What difference does it make if I do remember?" she asked at last. "Nothing has changed."

"Hasn't it?"

How could he ask such a thing? "Not the things that mattered. You are still holding back, as I must."

She ducked under his arm and ran up the steps on legs that shook, every nerve in her body humming with the awareness that he was right behind her. That he could, if he wanted to, catch her again. That she was right there on the verge of surrendering to passion. All over again.

This time she wasn't sure if she had the strength to stop herself from getting lost in his passion again. From losing her independence. Her sense of self-worth.

Dammit, she wouldn't be an emotional puppet like her mother, letting a man rule every aspect of her life. This was why she feared she would never be able to have that type of relationship again.

The photographer's gallery was the fourth level up and

she pushed inside without waiting for Marco. But she knew the instant he entered the shop behind her because her skin tingled, craving his touch again.

She shook off thoughts of him and took in the cramped gallery. Ivory plastered walls were covered with a multitude of framed photos ranging from breathtaking landscapes to the most realistic portraits she'd ever seen.

None were staged. In fact, the majority were candid shots. The range of emotion captured on the people's faces spoke to the feelings trapped inside her. Longing. Fear. Love.

"Look. That's Bella." Marco pointed to a framed photo set apart from the others as if it held a place of honor.

The young girl in the portrait stared down at them with guarded eyes. Eyes that looked far too old for her age.

Delanie pressed a hand to her heart, mouth dropping open. Marco had told her Bella had come from poverty but she'd never truly considered what that meant. She hadn't realized Bella had had to work as a child.

The picture showed stained clothes that hung on her small frame, her thin arms holding a large tray of fish draped with linen, the burden seeming too great for one so young and frail.

Heat swept up Delanie's cheeks, a burning wash of shame such as she'd never felt before. She hadn't had the ideal childhood, but she had been given every material convenience available. She hadn't had to work. Hadn't wanted for anything but frivolities.

"I just want to cry when I stare into her eyes," she said.

His palm rested on her lower back, softly, but this time she didn't jolt. Didn't pull away. This time she wanted this connection to him, wanted to share the agony and anger that coursed through him.

"Bella was twelve when Cabriotini's lawyer found her living with the fishmonger." His fingers splayed on her back and she couldn't help but lean into him. "Her mother had died three years before and he was her stepfather, the closest thing she had to family. He'd remarried but kept Bella, allowing her room and board in exchange for helping him in his shop."

She faced him, and her heart ached at the bleakness etched on his handsome face. He cared more than she'd thought possible. And if he was capable of caring that much for his sister...

As quickly as the thought popped into her head she pushed it away. She didn't dare let herself hope for more with him no matter how much compassion he showed his sister.

"At least they found her and got her out of that life," she said, her palm stroking the line of his clenched jaw, content for now to share this special moment with him. "What you've done for her, though, is wonderful. You gave her a home and family."

He snorted, relaxing marginally. "I did what Cabriotini should have done years before. He knew Bella was his daughter yet he did nothing to help her."

"Why?"

"Because she was female and a young unschooled one at that," he said.

Exactly what her own father would have done. Delanie had spent her whole life feeling second-rate because of her sex. Because her father had believed only a man could run his corporation.

But not Marco. He'd set his sister up as co-owner of Cabriotini Vineyard. He gave her the mansion, preferring his villa nestled in the hills.

And another misconception about Marco fell away, revealing a man with a big heart. With compassion. A man she could trust?

"May I help you?" a young man asked.

"I have an appointment with Carlo Domanti," she said.

The young man speared Marco an assessing look before turning back to her. "Delanie Tate, I presume?"

"Yes," she said, suddenly beset with nerves by the way this man boldly scrutinized her.

Marco thrust his hand out and introduced himself, offering no more than his name. If it rang a bell with Carlo, he didn't let on.

"That picture," Marco said, pointing to his sister. "I want it."

Carlo locked his arms over his chest. "It's not for sale."

"Everything has a price," Marco said.

She winced, all too aware that he'd found her price and used it to gain her compliance—in and out of bed.

The photographer's gaze narrowed on Marco. "Why do you want it?"

"That girl is my sister."

Carlo flung a hand in the air and spat out a stream of curses. "That is a lie! She does not have a brother."

"Bella didn't know about me then." Marco got right in the photographer's face. "I was unaware of her as well until several years after that picture was taken."

Carlo studied him, brow furrowed, arms locked over his chest. Finally he gave a nod, and Delanie blew out the breath she'd been holding.

"I will consider your offer," Carlo allowed, but it was obvious by his scowl that he wasn't convinced.

Marco's mouth hinted at a smile. "I assure you it will be a profitable deal for you."

If the photographer was tempted by money, he certainly hid it well. But at least the throbbing tension had eased enough for her to finalize this business.

"Mr. Domanti, I take it you know Bella?" Delanie asked.

The photographer bobbed his head. "We were born in the same village in the same questionable circumstances."

Bella's insistence that Delanie find this particular photographer made sense now. "Then you're long-time friends."

"I remember when she was born. As she was the only girl, I made it my duty to watch her the best I could. But she was rebellious. Stubborn. Proud. The last time I saw her, spoke to her, was when I took that photo." His gaze narrowed on Marco again. "I left her as she wished but I never forgot her. Where is she? Is she all right?"

"She is well and about to become a married woman," Marco said.

"That's why we're here. Bella wants you to photograph her wedding," Delanie said.

The photographer threaded long lean fingers through his mop of curly hair. "You work for Bella?"

"I do," Delanie said. "Now if we could sit down and nego-tiate the terms, number of photos…"

Carlo slashed the air with a hand, a gesture so reminiscent of Marco in a mood that she nearly laughed. It must be a uni-versal language for Italian men.

"I would do it for free for Bella," Carlo said.

"Bella wouldn't want that," Delanie said before Marco could interject anything.

Without further delay she quoted a figure well above the normal rate, all the while removing the contract from her port-folio. "If you would just read and sign this, we're all set to go."

Carlo didn't hesitate, giving her very straightforward con-tract a quick read. He signed it with an artistic flourish.

Moments later Marco was ushering her out the door, but not before he offered the photographer a staggering sum of money that was reluctantly accepted. All for that one poignant picture of Bella.

"It's touching that you want that portrait so badly," she said as they started down the stone stairs.

"There is nothing endearing about it. I don't ever want to forget the wrong done to us both," he said. "And I sure as hell don't want to risk it falling into the wrong hands either."

"Paparazzi?"

He gave a crisp nod. "In her condition, she doesn't need bad press and neither does her fiancé."

"I can't argue with that logic."

He stopped, forcing her to do the same. His mouth quirked in an utterly charming grin that sent her senses somersaulting.

"What? We are in agreement?"

She couldn't stop her smile, couldn't find a reason to pull away from him. "Surely it's a quirk of fate."

He laughed, a deep rich sound that coaxed her to do the same, to let loose with him. There had been few times when they'd laughed together, when they'd been this free and light of heart.

But as much as she reveled in his smile, his touch, as much as she yearned for his kiss, she knew she was treading on dangerous ground with him. She wasn't a starry-eyed young girl any longer.

She knew heartache followed sweet bliss, that as much as they meshed in bed, out of it they clashed. Now that she'd glimpsed another side of Marco, she was even more vulnerable to him.

"I'm anxious to tell Bella the news," she said, hoping he readily took her hint to leave Florence.

His smile was wide and totally unexpected. "You are making her dreams come true effortlessly. Bravo."

"Thank you."

They fell into step on the street, making their way through the growing crowd toward the Bugatti. Delanie smiled to herself. For a man who wanted to blend in, he certainly missed the boat by driving such a flashy car.

"What amuses you so?" he asked as he assisted her into the low passenger seat.

She spread her arms. "This. It's the red flag you wave in defiance of your attempt to remain the anonymous billionaire. Deep down you want to be noticed."

His smile fled, his body going painfully stiff in a blink. "You're wrong. Italian men adore performance cars. I own it because I can."

He shut the door soundly on the car and his emotions as well. Shutting her out.

She wet her dry lips, hesitant to follow him into his dark place. That had been their pattern but she was tired of it.

"You dreamed of owning a car like this when you were a boy working in the fields," she said after he slid behind the wheel and sent the Bugatti whizzing down a warren of narrow streets.

He cut her a look that was so boyish and charming she smiled. "It is true. The precise make and model don't matter but the flashy cars were always red. Always fast and always driven by the man who was in charge of his world."

"Then you have achieved your goals," she said.

He shrugged. "Not all."

What else could he want? A wife? Children? Love?

She refrained from probing. She didn't want to know how he intended to live his life after she returned to England. Didn't want to think about him losing his heart to another woman.

With effort, she focused on the reason she had come to Italy. Bella and her wedding. He would move mountains to please his sister and it was her job to make sure all went smoothly.

"Traditionally the father of the bride gives his daughter a special token on her wedding day," she said, sliding him a look to gauge his reaction. "It would be nice if you stepped into that role for her."

"I am giving her a vineyard and a villa," he said, jaw set.

She flexed her fingers when she longed to curl them into fists and pound the dashboard. "I was thinking of something more personal."

"It is that important?"

"Marco! Of course it is. This is your sister and she will hope to have a personal token from you to remember this special day."

"Ah, a memento." He frowned, nodded. "Very well. What should this gift be?"

She just caught herself from reaching out to him, from laying a commiserating hand on his arm. "A piece of jewelry would be lovely. Something for her to treasure."

"Good idea. We will visit Ponte Vecchio," he said.

Moments later he whipped the car down a narrow cobbled street and parked. But he didn't budge, save for the tightening of his fingers on the steering wheel as he stared at the gray buildings stacked neatly on top of each other. She wondered if he even noticed the people traversing the street, or if he was lost in some memory again.

What bothered him about this place? she wondered, seeing nothing remarkable or disturbing about Florence. It was a fairly large city but not nearly as hectic as London or Paris.

"Change your mind?" she asked.

"No, just thinking. Come."

He helped her leave the car and escorted her down the walkway toward the bridge. The closer they got to it, the more people they encountered. Yet his tension seemed to ease.

"What is this place?" she asked at last.

"This is the home of the most renowned goldsmiths in all of Italy. You will help me choose a gift," he said, smiling.

"I would be happy to."

The shops on the bridge were stuck together as if glued. It seemed as if no attempt had been made to make the buildings uniform in size, and several protruded over the deep blue river as if hanging on for dear life.

Delanie knew the feeling as she clung to Marco's hand, aware he was a powerful yet very tentative lifeline. As they strolled along the walkway with the stone wall to her right and shops clustering the Ponte Vecchio ahead, he told her the fascinating history of the goldsmiths of Florence extending back four hundred years.

She smiled, the sun warm on her face while a cool breeze

from the river whispered around her shoulders. Coupled with the enthusiastic man beside her it was a perfect moment, one she'd never thought she would share with him.

"I feel as if I'm in the company of a tour guide," she said, half teasing, but it coaxed another smile from him.

Her heart skipped a beat and warmed. Ah, such a very sexy, very handsome tour guide.

"How is it that you know so much about Florence?"

He shrugged, not that tense lifting of broad shoulders that he'd affected the past week, that she hated. No, this was the boyish hike that she found endearing and that hint of old pain she saw in his eyes showed a glimpse of the man she'd fallen so desperately in love with years ago.

And heaven help her but she was doing it again. She was utterly helpless to stop her heart from melting.

"My grandfather Vincienta owned a decanting shop on the edge of Florence. It was beyond the new bridge to the left." He pulled her to the wall and pointed downriver, but to her the land blended, all looking the same. Besides, she was more fascinated watching the emotions flickering like a movie on Marco's face, a face that was for once open and relaxed.

"Nonno wasn't a savvy businessmen. If a friend or a kind face wanted *vino* or *olio* and promised to pay later, he would give it to them on good faith. The debts mounted, so much so that my papa couldn't hold on to the shop after his father's death."

Marco gave a deprecating laugh, but it was the hand tightening on hers that made her flinch, not from pain but from the frustration that coursed from him into her. She sensed whatever change had happened then hadn't been a good one.

"Mama's father, Nonno Toligara, offered Papa a job in his small *olio* press and vineyard, but Papa got a better offer from Antonio Cabriotini. My mother begged Papa to refuse the offer but he took it anyway because he never wished to work for family again, especially not my grandfather who had not wanted him for a son-in-law in the first place."

"Was your father aware that you… I mean that you weren't his child?" she settled for, her voice hushed as they started across the bridge.

"According to my nonna, it was a year or more after he went to work for Cabriotini when Father discovered the truth, though my family still kept it from me. I did not understand why life at home changed. Why my parents fought more. Why my papa purposely spent less and less time in my company."

"How could he ostracize the child he'd raised since birth?" she asked, her other hand coming up to his arm, the muscle so tense she felt as if she were grasping a stone pillar.

He stopped in the lee of the arch leading onto the bridge, his gaze so bleak and pained she wanted to cry. "Papa held to old-world beliefs and I was a bastard in his eyes. A constant reminder of his wife's betrayal. Though they argued fiercely and he ignored me as much as possible, he never physically mistreated me. In fact, he did me a favor."

"How can you say that?"

"Papa discouraged me from working with him at Cabriotini's vineyard or for my Nonno Toligara. He insisted I get an education. That I learn business so I wouldn't repeat the mistakes of my ancestors," he said. "I balked at first, thinking if I worked with my father it would strengthen our relationship, that we would become close again. A few months after I began secondary school, my parents died in an auto accident and I was sent to Montiforte to live with my Nonni Toligara."

"That's so tragic," she said, a fist pressed to her heart.

One shoulder lifted. "Yes, but a blessing as well. They saw that I got an education, both at the winery and press and later at the university." His fingers tangled with hers. "Come."

What could she say to that? That they would be proud he'd done so well? That he'd done the impossible insofar as he'd regained the family business and made it far better?

It seemed wiser to keep those thoughts to herself as he led her onto the bridge, his hand tightly clasping hers. Ponte Vecchio teemed with people, from single shoppers to mothers with children to couples strolling hand-in-hand.

It was unlike any place she'd seen before. The vibrant colors of the awnings over some shops and the array of finery glistening in the line of windows left her as excited as a child at Christmas.

When they walked past the breaks between buildings, she caught a breathtaking view of the river winding though vineyards and olive groves painted in muted golds and bronze with the shadow of mountains in the distance. It was a vista painters coveted, yet her gaze was drawn time and again to Marco.

He stopped before a shop framed in wood, stained a rich patina by much polishing. A bank of bay windows overflowed with a stunning array of gold jewelry, its glow blinding in the late-day sun.

"This is the place," he said and dragged her inside.

Delanie craned her neck as she passed a glass case with the most dazzling array of gold bracelets, the size and intricate designs begging a second look. But the next showcase was just as stunning, just as breathtaking as the other.

Everywhere she looked, her gaze fell on the warm liquid sensuality of ultra-fine gold. Or on one arrogantly gorgeous Italian who had yet to release her hand.

"Is it really all eighteen-carat?" she asked Marco as he caught a clerk's eye.

"Yes, all the goldsmiths here pride themselves on selling the highest grade gold." He bent over a case. "Which one do you think Bella would like?"

She pointed to a display of pendants suspended on fine twisted gold chains. "Any of these freeform designs should appeal to her."

"I like the middle one," he said.

She smiled in agreement. "I think that will be perfect for your sister."

Marco nodded to the patient clerk and the older man hurried to comply. Delanie grasped the opportunity to put distance between her and Marco, to focus on the array of jewelry instead of on the doubts that were hammering away at her, an insistent ache that left her shaken inside, left her questioning everything to do with him.

How different her life would be if the lies hadn't gotten between them. If she had walked away from her business and her family. If she were his wife instead of his lover....

"You like?" Marco asked, appearing at her elbow with that same maddening stealth that had stolen her heart so long ago.

With effort she tore her gaze from the dark liquid languor glowing in his eyes to the warmth of the gold pendant suspended from an equally exquisite chain. "It's fabulous. I've never seen anything quite like the chain or the pendant."

"They are unique blends of modern design and fabled Florentine craftsmanship," he said, smiling, relaxed, his command of his world so appealing. "In many ways, the Etruscan influence still runs deeply here."

In the craftsmanship and the people? She'd read about the indigenous people while in school but had trouble dredging up any specifics. Not so for Marco.

But then he'd been born here. He'd been surrounded by this curious mix of old world and new most of his life. The rich cultural wealth that flowed alongside the Apennines coursed in his blood as well.

That only proved again how little she'd known about him ten years ago. How little she'd attempted to learn about his life.

Her cheeks heated as she admitted to herself that she'd been too selfish to think beyond her own world.

She bit her lower lip, the gold before her blurring into a liquid burnished sea. The life she'd wanted was close enough to taste, to embrace. So why did her heart ache at the thought of leaving here? Leaving Marco?

"Which piece would the lady like to see?" the clerk asked, appearing on the other side of the case as if by magic. As if expecting Marco to buy more of the lavishly expensive jewelry.

For her? Not on her life! She would make love with him but she would not take a token of gold back to London.

Her fingertips grazed the polished edge of the case, blinking frantically to disperse her sudden tears. "Nothing, thank you. I'm just window-shopping."

Marco edged closer, his arm touching hers lightly, yet sending her insides into a tumble all the same. "Come on. You must like one piece more than the other."

With Marco so close and behaving so charmingly again she was having trouble thinking straight. If she didn't know better, she would swear he was flirting with her. But that was preposterous. Wasn't it?

She rubbed her left temple, frustrated she couldn't concentrate on anything but Marco standing so close. His unique scent drifted in a silken glide over her skin, leaving her trembling.

Marco in his most arrogant persona she could deal with. But when he was like this, sweet, sexy, attentive, she couldn't think of anything but falling into his arms, holding him, kissing him, loving him. Dangerous thoughts to have for a man she intended to walk away from—for good this time.

"Can't decide?" he prodded.

With effort, she shook off the drugging effect that was totally him and pointed toward the pendant she'd been admiring earlier. Only as her vision cleared, she realized that the necklaces were no longer there.

She scanned the case, a frown pulling at her brow. When had the clerk exchanged the tray of pendants for rings?

The little man was quick to hold up a stunning ring for her inspection, carefully setting it on the velvet pillow. Her breath caught and her pulse raced. She'd never seen such delicate gold filigree or such an amazing rainbow of fire reflecting off one diamond.

"It's exquisite," she said.

The clerk made an appreciative sound. "Would the lady like to try it on?"

"No!" She pushed back from the case, glancing at Marco, then the door. "I'll wait outside for you."

With that she fled the shop and the sweet lure of the man she feared she would never forget.

CHAPTER NINE

MARCO credited a good deal of his swift success to the fact that he relied on his gut instincts. So far they hadn't let him down. He saw no reason to defer from that course now when the object of his desire was in sight.

Or more specifically, his desire was sitting beside him as he raced back to his villa. His suddenly silent, suddenly edgy object of desire.

There had been a major quake between them as they'd walked onto Ponte Vecchio. For some reason he had yet to understand, it had erupted in the jeweler's shop when the clerk assumed that Delanie was his fiancée and had trotted forth the tray of rings.

Delanie had been mellowing toward him all day, even giving him that look that was a green light aimed directly at him. Then, the second the clerk pulled up the engagement ring Delanie had been admiring, she had pulled away. She had actually run from the shop.

What madness had come over him to stand by and watch? Why hadn't he been the one to immediately pull her out of the shop when the engagement rings were trotted out, ending any speculation of what she meant to him?

Those questions nagged at him as he followed her out, finding her standing in the arched opening of the bridge, wind threading through her hair.

"What is wrong?" he'd asked, pulling her behind a pillar where they had a modicum of privacy.

"It was so hot in there," she said, her gaze turned to the river. "Didn't you notice?"

Then before he could reply, she'd slipped from him again and walked back to the stone railing. By the time he'd joined her, she was smiling, though he saw a note of strain around her expressive eyes and the lovely mouth that he longed to kiss.

"I love this view," she said.

"So do I." But he wasn't looking at the fertile hills or the haze of the Apennines in the distance.

He was staring at Delanie, his gaze worshiping her, devouring her. A sudden swift stab of longing twisted in his gut as he stared at her.

In less than a week now, Bella would be married and Delanie would expect him to make good on his deal with her. She would return to London with the success of a much-publicized wedding in her portfolio, in full control of her business.

Both of them would go on with their lives. Except he wasn't ready to see her go.

Though they shared a refreshing lunch later, all spontaneity was gone the moment they got in his Bugatti for the drive home. The closer they'd gotten to his villa the more remote she had become.

He flexed his fingers on the steering wheel, annoyed and frustrated. As they neared Montiforte, he sensed Delanie slipping away from him.

If he didn't do something to stop this soon, she would lock herself into some secret place that he couldn't reach. He would lose her again before he truly had her.

But what if she stayed? What role would she play in the life of a man who had sworn never to marry? Mistress?

No, she wouldn't do that. She wouldn't stay. So he had to make the most of this opportunity.

"Do you need anything from the village?" he asked.

"Everything is done and progressing on schedule," she said. "It's just a matter of checking in with the vendors and the bride daily until the wedding day."

Minutes later they were at his house nestled in the hills. Before they got out of his car, he knew exactly what he was going to do. There would be no altering it this time.

"Thank you for the lovely day," Delanie said as she stepped into the sunbathed patio.

"It was my pleasure."

He stopped in the doorway, shoulder braced on the jamb, gaze savoring the enticing view of her very firm, very sexy backside. His pulse kicked up, his groin tightening.

"You have done a remarkable job," he said.

"Thanks," she said, not slowing. Fleeing, nearly.

He flexed his fingers, aware there would be no going back, jaw firming with his decision. "We will celebrate your success tonight."

She came to a stiff halt by the chaise, hand gripping the plump backrest. "That isn't necessary."

"I disagree."

He pushed away from the door, crossing to her in three strides. His palms grazed her shoulders and he damned the silk that kept him from feeling the velvet of her bare skin.

"We need this celebration, Delanie. Just us," he said.

He heard her swallow and was startled to find his own throat felt just as tight, that his nerves were not as unruffled as usual. She did this to him, kept him off balance just that fraction, rocking the stable foundation he'd carved out.

No other woman had ever left him so on edge. Just Delanie. She'd done it from the first moment they'd met, when she'd given all to him that first time before letting fear choke her. He'd had no idea how to deal with it then.

He wasn't entirely sure now, but he knew passion churned deeply in her, passion that she felt for him. His fingertips tingled with the need to touch her, hold her, release that need in her that coursed through him as well. A whirlpool of unrest swirled in his gut, a gnawing hunger that only she could sate.

She faced him then, eyes wide and cheeks kissed with a rosy flush. "You want sex," she said frankly.

"I wanted you the moment I stepped onto Ponte Vecchio with you," he said, hand cupping her head, canting her face gently up to his. "Perhaps even sooner."

And then his lips were on hers, hot, ravenous. Flames exploded in his blood, a firestorm of desire that licked through his veins.

He slipped an arm around her narrow waist and pulled her flush against him, the sizzle in his blood popping like a champagne cork in his head.

His skin was on fire, the hot tips of her breasts branding his chest. Her scent was on him, in him, blotting out the world, blotting out everything but her. This moment. Them.

This is how it had been between them before. It was how it was meant to be: a fire of consuming need and blazing heat that they danced in when they were wrapped in each other's arms.

She was his. He knew it in his gut, his soul.

He only had to convince her of that. Coax her to soften, to surrender. To realize that this was where she was supposed to be.

With him. By his side. In his bed.

His lips traced the curve of her jaw, her slender neck, her delicate stubborn chin before settling over her sweet mouth in a kiss that sang through his veins. The rightness stealing over him dashed any doubts.

This was right. This was what should be. Surely she knew that. Felt the depth of emotions rejoicing within him.

She moaned, bowing into him as if to remind him how well their bodies fitted together. Not that he needed a reminder. He recalled every delicious moment he'd spent with her; the memories tormented his sleep.

Yet another sign she was the only woman for him. Yes, he'd had other lovers in the ensuing years. Lovely women he'd romanced. Women he'd treated well but who weren't around for long. Women who failed to compare to Delanie Tate.

Weeks after being with them, he had trouble remembering their faces. But not Delanie's.

He remembered everything. How her pupils darkened when they came together. Her breathy pants. Her touch, her scent, the beat of her heart against his.

He pulled back, breath sawing heavily, blood raging like a swollen river. "I want you, *cara mia.*"

"I want you as well," she said, the husk in her now-breathy voice the most erotic thing he'd ever heard.

He leaned back further, just enough to stare into the dreamy depths of her eyes, her pupils dilated, her lips plump and wet from his kisses.

He cupped her hips and yanked her against him, rocking his engorged shaft against her softness. "I want to make love with you until we are too weak to move, until we have freely spent our passion. And then, after we have rested, we will do it again. And again."

"Yes," she said, her voice a sexy huskiness that played over his senses in sweet abandon. "Let's make love all night long."

She flung her head back with a gasp and threaded her fingers through his hair, her nails scraping his scalp, the match to flint that sent a firestorm raging through his blood. Heat flared, roared through him with every erotic grind of her hips against his hard length.

Still she held part of herself back, denying him his conquest. And so he cast off his own reservations and kissed her with all the passion trapped inside him.

A moment passed, then another. Finally her very proper veneer went up in ash, revealing the earthy soul of a woman lost to abandon. Lost to him.

He gritted his teeth, sweat beading his brow as pressure

pounded through his veins so fiercely he feared he would explode. Feared the fire raging in him would burn him to a crisp.

Structured thoughts scattered under the blaze of desire sweeping over him. He could barely draw a decent breath, but he dug deep to clutch the cold steel in his spine to temper his lust. To hold on to a modicum of control.

His body ached for a quick tumble to ease the mountain of tension stacked inside him like the village houses against the hills. One fracture was all it would take to break free the desire he'd dammed up for too long.

Once would never be enough with her. A taste would only leave him hungering for more. And he would have it, a long sensual feast of the senses to last the night and beyond, to fog the issues he avoided with her, that he refused even to consider with another woman.

Her kisses turned wild, the rake of her fingernails stoking the fire in him. If he didn't know better, he would swear she was more ravenous for this than he was. Would think it had been far too long since she'd reveled in this sweet pleasure with a man. But that couldn't be.

Even if it were true he refused to dwell on it now. Thoughts of her with anyone but him were poison in his soul, dangerous and undermining.

She was in his arms now. Soon she would be in his bed where he intended to keep her until this driving need left him. A night, a day. Maybe two and this urgency would be gone.

For now he would enjoy her. For now she was his. For now they were together.

His fingers bit into the inviting curve of her hips covered in the slim tight skirt. "I will explode if I don't have you soon."

"It's okay," she said, nipping his chin while drilling the hard points of her nipples into his chest. "I can't wait much longer either."

He stripped off her blouse and skirt with hands that trembled, then helped her rip his shirt off his heated body, unable to bear her tender attempts. Though cool air whispered over his flesh he still burned deep for her.

When was the last time he'd been this desperate to possess a woman? Ten years ago, he thought without hesitation. Ten long years ago with the same enchanting woman.

The air crackled with electricity, making each touch a sensual jolt that left him trembling inside. He was burning up with unquenchable need, and the beautiful blush kissing her cheeks, neck and the full breasts that heaved in tempo with his ragged breaths told him that she wanted this just as much. Wanted him.

Yet he dragged out this long-awaited foreplay a bit longer by simply caressing her with his gaze. Knowing it would be sweeter in the end. Going as far as he dared, then pushing the boundary a bit more but finally taking her into his arms and kissing her, stroking his hands up and down her bare back.

Her hands were just as busy, sliding down his sides, her fingertips skipping over the firm globes of his bottom. An avalanche of sensations zipped over his heated skin and he faltered, tossing his head back to gasp for air.

"You are magnificent," she said, clutching his length with small knowing hands that threatened to bring him to his knees.

"*Cara,*" he said on a hiss, afraid to breathe, to move for fear she would stop. "You are killing me."

"Softly comes this death," she said, kneeling before him, fingers still worshipping his sex.

Then her mouth touched him there, the shock so electric he jolted. Perhaps cursed. Perhaps said a prayer as her lips trailed up and down his length until he wanted to howl with the pleasure thundering through him.

He treaded his fingers through her silken hair, holding her close, straining for control that was fast spiraling away from him.

This was sweet erotic torture, and it was something he never allowed for it put the woman in control. It stole the power from him. Stole rational thought and replaced it with earthy need.

But he'd taught her this soon after they met, encouraged her to explore him because he'd thought it would loosen her inhibitions. It had to a degree, but she'd relished the control, her ability to give him pleasure while holding back giving her all to him in turn.

That had begun the pattern of their intimacy that had kept them apart, that would throw up a wall between them now unless she totally surrendered herself to him.

So he held back now, tense muscles jerking with the hunger for pleasure. His skin burned, too hot, too tight, certain to break if he didn't find release soon.

It would not be this way.

That was the lone thought on his mind as he dug deep and found the strength to stop this sweet torture.

"Not now." He jerked her to her feet and dragged her flush against him.

"But…"

He silenced her protest with a kiss that conquered. Demanded.

She hesitated. Stiff, caught off guard. Then a sound bubbled from the back of her throat and she met his kiss with equal fervor.

He slid his palms over her sexy bottom and trailed his fingers down her thighs. The cool silk of her tender skin sent a shiver rocketing through him.

His blood hammered so loudly he felt rather than heard her needy moan. But he gave her no rest, stroking the delicious curve of her hips, the lush fullness of her bottom, the slick seductive folds between her trembling legs.

"Oh, God," she said, clutching his shoulders, back bowing to push her bosom and sex closer to him.

"Yes," he said thickly, coaxing her on with deeper strokes

of his fingers and trying like hell to hold his own desire in check.

It was hell and heaven, extracting more stamina from him than he thought was possible. His limbs ached, his muscles knotted. Sweat poured off his brow and down his back. His sex throbbed, ready to burst.

"Marco!"

"Let go, Delanie. Let go like you did the first time."

"I can't," she said, voice cracking.

"You can. Do it. You won't regret it, *cara*."

He held her as passion warred with her fear, as her fingers dug into his shoulders, her gaze locked with his. Triumph surged through him as desire finally glazed her eyes, as her lovely body rippled in erotic surrender and his patience paid off tenfold.

It had been too long since he'd enjoyed watching a woman reach her passion. Too long since he'd felt this sense of awe. Too long since he'd been gifted with Delanie's full passion.

Her fingernails dug into his flesh so hard she likely drew blood but he didn't care. His lips curled in male satisfaction, chest puffing with the assurance that he'd been the one to give her such pleasure. That he'd gained the same just watching desire sweep her up in its honeyed maelstrom.

The strength of her climax left her in sated bliss and he caught her, cradled her close. But what caught him by surprise was the swelling of his heart, the warmth that stole over him as he looked down at her, a rightness that was unlike anything he'd felt before, even with her.

A thread of fear pulled through him and tightened his gut. He didn't want to feel emotion this deeply. Didn't want those tender emotions clawing at him, trying to burrow in.

What he'd had with Delanie was history. This was their time to part amiably. To be adults and admit there never would be any future for them together. To savor each other and this moment.

He blocked everything from his mind but the fact he was overly aroused and had a very naked, very willing woman in his arms. This was sex and he would make sure it was the best sex either of them had ever had.

They would part without regret before the wedding. The past would be just a fond memory.

"I can't wait," he said, setting her on the counter, the bedroom simply too great a distance in his condition.

Her legs parted in invitation and her fingers dug into his shoulders. "Neither can I."

He pulled her forward and thrust into her, and a deep satisfied growl rumbled from him. Being in her wasn't enough. He had to kiss her. Had to parallel the sensual assault with his mouth. Had to hold her and stroke her soft flesh.

But he sensed no complaint. Nothing but sweet surrender.

The last was something he never allowed in a lover. But this was Delanie. This was something that was reserved only for her. That he'd waited to experience for far too long.

They were both lost in desire, their bodies moving in rhythm, knowing where to stroke, to touch, to bring the most pleasure.

It vaguely occurred to him that they were equally dominant now. That they were in perfect sensual sync. He took, she gave, and vice versa.

They were matched. Perfect together?

That was the last thought on his mind as she climaxed and he gave over as well. The lone thought that locked his knees and kept him standing as wave after wave of pleasure coursed through him.

She clung to him, limp, sated. He laid his face aside hers, his breath tortured as he fought to regain sanity after the little death.

And he *had* lost his sanity, he realized, as he slowly eased from her. When had he been this irresponsibly horny?

"Dammit," he hissed, muscles taut with anger.

"What's wrong?" she asked, her voice having a drowsy, sexy edge that was making him hard again.

"We—" He pursed his lips and made a slicing motion with his hand. "I didn't think to use protection."

Which brought a whole host of what-ifs into play, foremost being what if he got her pregnant? The answer was obvious. He would not sire a bastard. No way. They would have to marry and pronto.

Her hands slid around his hot, tense nape. "It's all right. I'm on the pill and I assure you I'm clean."

His breath left him in a whoosh, taking the tight coil of tension with it. She was protected. Not trying to trap him into marriage.

"That," he said, kissing her forehead, her nose, "is very good to know."

"I thought you would approve," she whispered against his neck. "That was bloody awesome. In case you're wondering, once won't be enough."

He tipped his head back and laughed, something else that he never did with a woman after sex. Delanie joined him, free, relaxed.

No strings. No commitments. Just pleasure. That was all this was. So why did he feel a moment's annoyance? Why was he a bit disappointed to hear she'd had the foresight to protect herself against pregnancy?

He shrugged off the damned doubts that had no place in this moment. "This time, we will make good use of the bed."

This time, on legs that thankfully didn't shake, he carried her into the bedroom and proceeded to show her how much he enjoyed every delicious inch of her.

Delanie stirred, stretching like a lazy kitten. A twinge of discomfort streaked across her hipbones and she winced, stilling until the moment passed.

It had been this way every morning for the past three days,

each day and night spent in sensual wonder, each new day better than the one before.

Last night had certainly been no exception. She pinched her eyes shut, face heating to an uncomfortable warmth as each delicious minute flashed before her eyes.

They had made love well into the wee hours of the morning, not pounding urgent coupling but a slow, deep coming together that touched something in her she wasn't even aware of. Sometime in the early hours of the morning they'd finally fallen into an exhausted sleep.

She'd never felt closer to him. Never been so close to giving up anything and everything for him.

Yet Marco had left their bed before dawn. Perhaps he was on the terrace drinking coffee.

Or, she thought as she slipped from the bed, he was in his office working.

She would have enjoyed indulging in a hot bath but she needed to find Marco first. Talk to him. Gauge his mood.

In moments she was dressed in jeans and a lightweight sweater, attire perfect for a day spent here at the house. She padded to the door, wincing again at the tenderness between her legs and the abrasive rub of her lace bra against her nipples.

Her nerves tautened as she stepped into the kitchen, where the doors were thrown open to let in a gentle breeze. Her gaze took in the open area and the salon beyond. No sign of him.

Then, distantly, she heard the low rumble of Marco's voice drifting to her on the breeze. He was outside, speaking to someone in Italian.

She strode to the door and paused, catching sight of him pacing the length of the terrace, his mobile phone pressed to his ear. Words flew from him like bullets. Though Delanie couldn't keep up with the conversation, she sensed by his clipped tone that he was upset.

"Okay," Marco said, free hand fisted at his side. "Tell her I will be there in a few minutes."

Her stomach knotted as much from the tension in his voice as the fact he would leave the villa soon. So much for expecting an intimate morning together.

But then the timing of such things was rarely left to the mistress, she supposed. He would come in. Tell her about his change of plans and she would see him when it was convenient for him. Not her.

She crossed to the kitchen and splashed coffee in a cup, needing the caffeine jolt to her system. Though she'd intended to adopt a cosmopolitan demeanor regarding their affair, she simply couldn't do it.

It wasn't even a hard admission to make. She'd known from the start that she couldn't regard sex with Marco as a casual thing, especially if she stopped holding part of herself back. But there was no graceful way out now.

Her shoulders bowed as she walked toward the door, a smile trembling on her lips as she stepped out onto the terrace. A very empty terrace. Empty garden. Empty pool area.

She frowned. He hadn't come back into the house. Had he zipped off in his red sports car without a goodbye? Without a word to her?

That was simply unacceptable behavior! She set her cup of coffee down beside his half-drunk one and rounded the house, thinking she just might catch a glimpse of him peeling down the winding drive in his sleek red auto toward the "she" who needed him so much. But the Bugatti was right where Marco had parked it last night.

Baffled, she retraced her steps to the terrace. Just as she was ready to turn toward the door, she caught a blinding flash of white moving in the hills above the house.

She shielded her eyes and focused on the figure.

Marco? Yes, the more she watched the more sure she was of it. He was taking the trail upward and would soon be out of sight. Who was he going to see? Whose call had the power to send him out like this on foot?

A female neighbor in need perhaps? A convenient lover?

Delanie fisted her hands, welcoming the swift jab of anger that finally prodded her feet to move. She was well onto the track winding into the hills before it struck her that the wisest course was to fob this off and leave him to whatever lady had snared his fancy.

But curiosity was a cruel companion to jealousy and both were playing hell with her emotions right now. So she struck out after him, determined to find out where he'd gone in such a rush that he couldn't even leave her a note.

Staying on the well-maintained trail took her to a lovely clearing a good two kilometers above Marco's house. The stands of cypress and perfect lines of lofty poplars kept this little area well secluded, the perfect place to secrete away a mistress.

Her gaze took in the small farmstead. Instead of livestock, which she hadn't expected to find anyway, her gaze lit on several dozen medium-sized lanky dogs lazing in a fenced enclosure.

A woman with a dog kennel was the last thing she'd expected to find. How odd she'd never heard more than a few barks in all the time she'd been here.

She looked toward the barn, which she guessed was the heart of the operation, and just caught sight of Marco going inside. Without thinking that she was now trespassing or at the least spying on her lover, she struck out toward the barn as well.

Her heart was racing like the wind long before she stepped inside a small room furnished with a half dozen utility chairs and a counter that looked suspiciously like a reception area of sorts. She followed Marco's voice into the adjacent room where he knelt beside a tan dog. A woman of modest years with a stern countenance stood behind him with a perplexed look on her face.

"How long has she been like this?" Marco asked, brow furrowed as he ran a gentle hand over the dog's sleek coat.

"I found her this way this morning," the woman said. "The knee is completely displaced. Surgery might give her full range of movement again but at her age…"

Marco flung the woman a glacial look that made Delanie shiver. "Then operate. I have made it clear that Rifugio del Cuccia was built for the animals and that means prolonging their quality of life as long as it is humanly possible."

"Very well," the woman said. "I will operate on her this afternoon."

The woman walked off but Marco remained crouched by the animal. He stroked the dog gently and crooned so softly Delanie had to strain to hear the soothing melody, so rich and warm she pressed a hand to her mouth to stifle a sigh.

But the old greyhound responded, giving a weary wag of her tail. The dog lifted her head once to look at him before moaning and lying back down with a contented sigh.

Delanie's throat tightened and her eyes misted. And her heart… Oh, God, her heart flooded with warmth.

The animal loved him and he was clearly protective of the dog. Yet she never recalled him talking of animals the entire time she had known him. Just another slice of Marco Vincienta that he kept hidden from the world. A very compassionate side that she'd never seen to this degree.

She eased back toward the door, feeling very shallow for the earlier negative thoughts that had consumed her, compelling her to follow him. Feeling far too weak-kneed as well.

What she wouldn't give if he would show that much love to her!

But he couldn't. Or wouldn't.

She'd known from the start that leaving him would hurt.
That she still loved him.

But she hadn't realized until this moment that walking
away from this wonderful man would surely kill her.

CHAPTER TEN

"You don't have to leave," Marco said, still not looking up. "I'm not going to bite your head off for following me."

She grimaced. Another second and she would have been gone. Instead she scrambled for composure and a steady tone.

"No, you'll just sic the dogs on me," she said, aiming for a tease.

To her relief he smiled, a boyish grin that made her heart thump harder. "There's not a vicious one in the kennel, *cara*."

Again, she saw a different side of Marco as she crouched on the floor in a kennel making light conversation. The tension that had bonded to her suddenly came unglued. She shivered at the naked freedom of losing the encumbrance, of allowing herself to simply relax around him again.

An odd thing to admit after the intimacies they'd shared last night. She chafed her upper arms and glanced at her surroundings.

Kennels side by side down the perimeter, separated from each other by solid walls, had pet doors that opened into the fenced yard. A few dogs dozed in their cages but none as listlessly as the greyhound sprawled at Marco's feet.

"I didn't mean to intrude on a private moment," she said.

"You're not. I should have invited you to come with me," he said. "At the least, I should have told you why I had to rush off."

But he hadn't. His thoughts had been on the dog he obviously cared for instead of the woman he'd romanced all night.

Yet she couldn't fault him.

"It's all right. I take it this place is yours," she said.

He gave a crisp nod. "I bought this old farm several years ago and refurbished it into the dog kennel you see it today." His hand stilled on the listless greyhound, his smile tender. "Zena was one of our first guests."

"She's special to you then."

"Yes, but not like you think." He continued to pet the dog, seeming in no hurry to move or avoid her questions. "She was a champion, setting records with the amount of races she won in four years and deserves a luxurious retirement."

She shifted, her smile fading. "I wasn't aware you were involved in dog-racing."

Dark, narrowed eyes drilled into her and a muscle jerked along his jaw. "I never have been, at least not as a proponent of the sport. Their less-than-humane practices to the animals sickens me. The dogs earn billions for their owners yet are treated abominably. That is part of the reason I built this rescue shelter."

Zena moaned and lifted her head and Marco instantly focused his attention on the animal. The dog responded by stilling with a weary exhalation.

His broad shoulders relaxed, his hard features softened. It was all she could do to keep from going to him, rubbing the taut muscles, soothing him as he was comforting the dog.

"I just assumed…" She rubbed the chill from her arms again. "My apologies."

That earned her a negligent shrug. "It's ok. You made the same assumption most make considering my biological father had a penchant for gambling."

Delanie bit her lip, debating whether to let the subject drop or pursue it. There was certainly more to it. More that bothered him or else he wouldn't have gone to all this expense.

Wouldn't have been so emotionally invested in building a shelter just moments from his home.

"Do you mind if I join you?" she asked.

"Please, sit," he said, and the dog did no more than cast big brown eyes her way. Eyes that had clearly seen too much hurt and very little of the affection she was reaping now.

She bit her lip as she eased down on the other side of Zena. "I've never been around dogs."

He looked up. "You never had a pet?"

An image of chasing a dog flickered in her memory. "Mother was given a puppy once. He looked like a puff of fur and was so soft and so full of life." Too full of life for her household.

"What happened to him?"

She frowned at her clasped hands. "Father told us he had to find a new home for the dog because his allergies prevented close contact with animals of any kind."

He snorted. "Did you believe him?"

"Back then I did," she said. "But now? No."

Her gaze lifted from the dog to the man and her breath caught as her gaze locked with his dark somber eyes. The last thing she needed now was his compassion.

"What about you?" she asked. "Did you grow up around animals?"

"We had a dog when I was a boy. A mongrel, really."

He cracked a smile and her heart ached as she imagined him playing in the streets of Florence with his pet. Ached because she envied him that memory when her own was so fleeting.

"Tell me about your dog," she said. "What was his name?

"Sebastian," he said. "He followed me home from school one day, so scrawny he was little more than matted fur over bones."

"So you took him in," she said.

"Yes. Mama gave him scraps and he made himself at home on our back stoop."

His features softened, his eyes glowed, as he launched into a slice of life about a poor Italian boy on the winding cobbled streets in Florence, running with a mutt of a dog. Laughing. Free. Enjoying his childhood with parents who were passionately close at that time.

A gnawing pain that was simply jealousy for what he'd had and she hadn't popped up in her, as ugly as a sudden pimple on a cheek or chin. A mark to ignore or treat, and she struggled to do either.

At one time she'd pitied him for the dire straits he'd come from. But in truth it was she who'd lived in emotional poverty in the mansion in Mayfair. No matter how hard she tried she couldn't remember her mother and father laughing, together or apart. Couldn't remember the wealthy Tate family doing anything for the sheer enjoyment of it.

The only time she'd truly lived was when she'd met Marco. He'd pulled her out of her staid life and showed her a world bright with promise. He'd been exciting and loving and powerful.

When he'd left her, she'd retreated to what she'd known—protecting her mother as best as she could. Enduring.

Her budding career as a wedding planner became her only outlet. Through it she lived vicariously, enjoying others' happiness without risking her own heart again.

Sitting with Marco on the floor of a fabulous dog shelter terrified her more than she wished to admit. Her heart beat too fast, her thoughts whirled like a tempest, all centered around the man who had stormed back into her life and forced her really to look at her existence.

Gaining her independence had been all she'd wanted for so long. It still was her goal.

Entertaining thoughts of Marco remaining in her life was moot. Nothing had changed between them.

She deserved more than a one-sided affair of the heart. He couldn't open his heart to love. Or was there hope that would change?

That thought remained front and center in her mind as she reached out to stroke the dog. The stiff coat was surprisingly soft, much like Marco: He projected a hard exterior but clearly had a much softer spot in his heart for animals.

The dog was a breathing, needy connection between them because it was safer to touch the dog than each other. Safer than opening herself up to those feelings that were already battering down the door she'd locked them behind.

"I'm jealous of your memories of a happy home and family," she said.

He shrugged, and she coveted even that careless surety he affected without effort. "I have good ones and not so good ones. There are more chapters of the latter than the former."

"Mine range from bad to indifferent," she said, though she suspected her bad memories outweighed his. "But you had more than just parents at odds. My maternal grandparents died long before I was born. My father was estranged from his family."

He frowned. "So you were cut off from kin?"

She nodded. "Henry sent word to a younger sibling of Father's upon his death, but they didn't respond."

"That's wrong."

"Perhaps, but it was proof that Father reaped what he'd sown with family and business associates," she said.

She was spared saying more as the veterinarian strode into the room, her dark blue surgical scrubs a sign she was ready to operate. The woman didn't spare Delanie a glance.

"Marco, we are ready for Zena," the veterinarian said.

He shifted to a squat, his gaze on the dog as Delanie rose to her feet. "Should I carry her for you?"

"Grazie." The veterinarian held the door open. "Bring her in here, please."

He gently lifted the dog in his strong arms and disappeared through the door with the veterinarian trailing him. The metal panel closed with a clang.

Delanie paced the room and rubbed her bare arms again, debating whether to stay or to go back to the villa. She had no desire to witness a surgery though she suspected Marco would remain here until Zena was on the road to recovery.

She slipped out the door and headed to the path that wound back to Marco's house. Yes, she was running away, even though she couldn't run far from her troubles.

Once Marco had time for her, he would seek her out. Wine her. Dine her. Seduce her until she begged him to make love to her—to ease the torment of desire.

And when they'd rested, she would welcome his passion all over again.

Stolen days of bliss, that's all she had with him.

Halfway down the hill she paused at the breathtaking vista of Montiforte far below. She drank in the beauty like one famished, convinced she would never tire of letting her gaze wander the hills and quaint villages where hustle and bustle were foreign concepts.

How odd that she, the girl who had craved the excitement of London, would come to appreciate the quiet beauty of this landlocked part of Italy. Not once had she pined for her typical breakneck routine that was mired in the city. She had rarely thought of her friends.

An anomaly.

She'd been busy planning the wedding, getting to know the village and the people who were always quick to help. Then she'd gotten caught up in Marco's charisma, lost in his arms, addicted to his passion.

Too soon it would all end and she would return to her world. She would have the company she'd sacrificed years of her life to regain. She would lose Marco all over again.

Her shoulders slumped, her stomach knotting. Why

couldn't her heart race with excitement over finally gaining what she wanted? Why was the world she'd known less appealing than this laid-back lifestyle?

"It's a beautiful sight, no?" Marco said.

She let out a yelp, startled he'd sneaked up on her. "I thought you would stay with Zena."

He shook his head. "She is in good hands." His gaze roamed her length, as intimate as a caress. "What are your plans for today?"

"I have none," she said.

He slipped an arm around her, pulled her into the heat and hardness of his body and she melted against him effortlessly. Her heart leapt to life, thudding hard in her chest. Her breasts grew heavy, the nipples peaking to aching awareness.

"Then let's return to the house and enjoy the time left us. Okay?" he asked.

Asked!

She smiled and hoped he couldn't tell it was pained.

He offered the one thing he could give her without reservations. With total honesty. Passion.

Denying herself the pleasure wouldn't make leaving him any easier. A heart couldn't break any more than it had, could it?

"How can I say no?" she said.

Something had changed between him and Delanie in the shelter and damned if he could put his finger on it. But he didn't like it.

Her smile was just as warm as the sun. Her fingers still clung to his with the same urgency. Her eyes still burned with passion.

Yet he felt the distancing between them as if she were leaving him now instead of in a few days. That would come soon enough. For now, while he had her here they would make the most of their time together.

He would know for sure before she left him again if his pride had cost him the most important thing in his life.

"That sweet spicy smell. Is it coming from that flower over there?" she asked, pointing to a light purple bloom that had newly unfurled its petals.

"Yes, the much-prized *zafferano*," he said, and at her pulled brow added, "Saffron. It grows wild here and has been a major export for centuries."

"It's so delicate."

Much like Delanie, he thought, smiling. "Ah, but she is stingy with her treasure. *Zafferano* is the world's most expensive herb."

"Our chef made saffron rice," she said.

He snorted. "As does the world. But a saffron risotto with cinnamon pork—" He kissed his thumb and forefinger. *"Delizioso."*

Her kissable mouth pulled into a playful smile but it was the fingers tightening on his that sent a surge of heat blazing through him. "Okay, where do I sample this delicacy?"

One jerk brought her slamming against him, full lush breasts to hard heaving chest. He kissed her mouth quickly, then swooped back for another one, longer this time, lingering over her as one would a scrumptious dish.

"At my house, of course," he said, his voice thickened with his growing need to have her. Not any woman. Her. "With a stop in the village for ingredients."

"Who is going to cook this delicacy?" she asked as he inched toward the crocus and plucked off the three reddish stigmas.

He held such a treasure, yet it paled in comparison to the woman. She was the rare treasure.

"Me, of course," he said as he picked his way back to the trail, careful not to tread on new tender shoots. "I am not just a pretty face!"

She laughed, a rich playful sound that lifted the weight of

worry from him. They had this. The spontaneity of lovers that had not faded with time. But was it enough?

It had to be.

Delanie Tate wanted love. Wanted hearts and flowers. Wanted a man who would let her spread her wings and fly independently of him.

Marco simply couldn't do that. He couldn't allay his doubts that she would return to her lies. That in the end, she would find a man more dashing, more amiable than he and would betray him.

No, all he had with her was her time in Italy planning Bella's wedding. He intended to make the most of it.

He pressed a fortune's worth of fresh herb into her hands. "I will have you know that one of my early apprenticeships was cooking, and I was damned good at it."

"You're good at everything," she said with a smile.

If only he could be.... But nothing had changed.

"I am just a simple Italian," he said, and she laughed harder.

"There is nothing simple about you," she said, her teasing smile a balm to his doubts.

Hand in hand, they wound their way to the house, stopping for the occasional kiss. Each one lasted longer, firing his blood and numbing his mind well before they left the trail.

A drive to the village netted a selection of vegetables, a loaf of crusty bread and cuts of prime pork.

"You're serious about cooking for us," she said.

"Very. I will make a risotto that will melt in your mouth," he promised on the short drive back to the house.

"I'm embarrassed to admit I'm horribly inadequate in the culinary arts," she said, helping him carry their fare into the house. "Did your mother teach you?"

He smiled at that thought and poured two glasses of rich sagrantino. "My nonna taught me. She was an amazing cook. An amazing woman with only one fault—she was too trusting."

Her eyes swam with intense hurt, but it was the touch of

her fingers urgently gripping his hand that made his heart lurch. "I'm so sorry my father maliciously destroyed your family's business."

He shrugged, the fury that usually swept over him thankfully absent, leaving only the slow burn of deceit on his tongue. "I am too. But it's over. He is dead. The winery and olive press are mine again. And you are here with me."

She bit her lower lip and he caught the barest tremor shaking her before she managed a smile. "I'm glad we had this time together. That we've cleared the air of misconceptions."

His hand closed over hers, his pulse gaining speed as he stepped closer and cupped her cheek with his other palm. Her gaze lifted to his—open, questioning. Hesitant?

"Our affair doesn't have to be temporary."

She wet her lips, the pulse in her throat fluttering as wildly as his own. "Yes, it must end. Unless your feelings toward me have changed."

He couldn't breathe, couldn't think beyond the fact she'd called his hand, that she expected a declaration of his feelings before she would consider staying here.

It's what he'd known she would do all along. So why had he brought it up when he knew the answer would push them further apart?

"Nothing has changed," he said honestly, dropping a kiss on her nose, her chin, her mouth. "Especially not my hunger for you."

She held herself stiffly for a moment, then lifted her face to his. Was that a flicker of pain in her eyes?

He couldn't tell, and she drove the question from his mind by threading her fingers at his nape, bowing her body into his length. She kissed his chin, then nipped the flesh, sending a flash fire of desire racing through his blood.

"Then I suggest we enjoy good food and each other," she said, definitely taking the lead this time.

He ran a hand down her back, damning the soft barrier of clothes that kept him from caressing her silken skin, dragging her body flush against his with an urgency that totally lacked finesse. His mouth settled on hers, as hot and hungry as he'd been for her years ago. Maybe more so because having her again was better than a memory, richer, hotter.

She was a fire in his blood, making him burn from the inside out. His shirt clung to his slick back and chest. His jeans were a nagging constraint to his sex.

"We have on far too many clothes," he said, tearing his shirt off and flinging it aside.

"Way too many," she said, her voice a breathy huskiness that fired his libido another notch.

She raked her nails down his chest to his waistband, the white-lacquered tips he liked to see against his darker skin slipping beneath to graze the tip of his erection. He hissed in a breath and went still, praying for control.

"I am too full with want for you," he said.

"It's okay," she said, dragging his jeans down and kneeling before him. "I feel the same."

"Maledetto!" he hissed as her lips skimmed his hot hard length, her small fingers urgent on his skin.

He locked his knees and tipped his head back, giving her free rein, knowing by the blood roaring in his ears and pounding through his veins that it would be brief. The first part of his release jolted through him, his fingers threading through her hair as a shout exploded from him.

Somehow he remained standing until the last tremor rocked through him. He pulled her up into his arms, crushing her against his chest.

"You are a vixen."

"And you are a sorcerer, catching me up in your spell."

If only I could, he thought.

If he had that power, this would be the beginning instead of an interlude. She would be his forever.

He pushed the nagging thought from his mind. A flick of his fingers released the snap of jeans that hugged her rounded bottom as he'd longed to do on the long walk back to the house. But they were too snug to drop on their own. Like skin. Hot. More arousing than any model he'd seen, than any woman he'd ever crossed paths with.

He should forbid Delanie to ever wear them in public, he thought as he hooked his thumbs over the band and peeled them down, his skin riding her hipbones, catching the tiny band of her thong as well.

Sweat beaded his forehead, his chest warming quickly as well. Had sex ever been this erotic before? This much sensual torture?

He didn't know. Couldn't remember. But his sex jolted again, aching with the need to be in her.

"I love this," she said.

His ego swelled, his thoughts blurring in a haze of lust. He hoisted her onto the counter and spread her long sexy legs by riding his palms up her thighs, nostrils flaring as he caught her scent, insides tightening as she opened to him like a rose kissed by the morning sun.

"That is because this is heaven," he said, whisking her top and bra off and filling his palms with the creamy swells of her breasts, convinced this was as close to paradise as he would ever get.

His first flick of his tongue over a hardened peach nipple had her surging forward, wrapping her legs around his hips. The jolt of her moist sex against his belly shocked his system while pumping moisture to his engorged tip.

Yes, foreplay was over.

He cupped her lush bottom and slid her close, mouth bonding with hers in an explosion of raw lust. White lights exploded from their touch, blazing red as his sex found her wet, hot core and thrust in hard.

The world stopped for an instant, electricity streaking up and down his length, holding him in that erotic chasm for an instant. Heaven and hell.

No woman had ever brought him to such heights, made him feel so intently. He hated it as much as he craved it, ached for it.

She climaxed first, screaming his name. His hoarse shout, a benediction, a curse, he didn't know, burst from him a heartbeat later.

All thought left him then, replaced by a torrent of sensations that roared through him with cataclysmic force.

"Marco," she whispered against his shoulder, her hands clutching him tightly as if she feared she would tumble off the earth if she didn't hold on.

"I have you," he managed to get out, dredging deep to find the stamina he needed to carry the most precious thing he'd ever held in his hands.

Delanie. To his bedroom.

Each step was agony, taking a lifetime. But he got there and collapsed with her on the bed.

"You are amazing," she said and planted a kiss on his temple, lips sliding down his cheek even while her small hand sought and found his sex. "Amazing."

She made him believe that perhaps he was when blood rushed again to that part of him. The lethargy that had bound him was cut free, replaced by the beginning surge of desire.

He smoothed hands that shook just a fraction down her back, savoring the curve of her hip, the firm globes that filled out her jeans so very well. "I intend to spend every day I have with you right here."

"Good plan," she said, kissing her way past his belly, sliding lower to find his length that pulsed with need.

All rational thought fled him then, replaced by a nirvana he had known too seldom. But it felt right.

Everything felt right with Delanie.

No matter what, he damned sure wasn't letting Delanie go this time.

A week had never passed so pleasurably or quickly. They ate, they drank, they made love.

On the morning of the wedding, Delanie couldn't believe it was over. Didn't want to face the fact that their idyll was history.

Her contract would soon be satisfied and her affair with Marco would end. And then the heartache would truly set in.

She pressed a hand to the gnawing ache in her stomach. The only way she would be able to get through this day was to stay busy and stay away from Marco. So far so good.

But then, she thought as she stepped from the guest shower, he'd yet to rouse from their bed.

She dressed quickly in a beige shirtdress that was comfortable yet stylish enough to get her through the morning. Winding her still-damp hair in a French twist sufficed, and a bit of mascara helped divert attention away from the red streaks in her eyes. A bit of blush gave her unusually pale cheeks much-needed color.

So did the red patent belt she cinched around her waist. Stepping into matching red patent pumps and adding a strand of red beads with matching earrings completed her business attire.

"You are up at an ungodly early hour," Marco said.

She gasped, shaken to see him lounging against the doorjamb, his dark eyes unreadable, his jaw rigid. How long had he been watching?

"Today is the wedding so it is a workday for me."

He snorted. "Your bag looks packed."

"For the most part," she said. "I wanted as much done now as I could since I'll be busy all day."

There was nothing welcoming about the muscular arms crossed tightly over his bare chest either. Strong arms that had held her close to his heart last night, that were now hard with tension.

Her gaze followed the dark hair that arrowed over his washboard abs, disappearing under faded jeans that rode indecently low on his lean hips. How could he look angry and sexy at the same time?

"Why are you doing this, *cara?*"

"Because my job will be completed and there is no reason to remain in Italy any longer."

He muttered something in Italian that she couldn't guess. Just as well, for it was likely a curse.

"There most certainly is a reason." He waved a hand between them. "This thing between us is not over."

So close to the words she'd longed to hear. But she didn't want *close* anymore. She wanted the words, wanted to hear passion and his heart behind them.

All or nothing.

"This thing?" she repeated, and he jerked his hand back and stared at some point beyond her. "Can't you call it what it is? A love affair? Or is using the world *love* as much a problem for you as professing what's in your heart?"

His impossibly broad shoulders stiffened with military precision. His eyes burned with something she'd never seen before—an emotion that left her shaking inside.

"Love is nothing more than a word to me," he said. "A word without substance. A word that deceives."

She lifted a hand, right on the verge of reaching for him. Of cupping the jaw set like stone. Rubbing a thumb over lips that were pulled into a thin disagreeable line.

But she reined that impulse in and reached for her bag of

toiletries instead. She tossed them in her case with hands that shook, and she blinked her suddenly stinging eyes, desperate to stay the tears that threatened.

Crying would solve nothing. She'd learned that long ago.

"You're wrong, Marco," she said. "But until you stop fearing the emotion that can free you, you'll never believe in its power. There will always be something missing from your life, something you can't buy or take over."

He snorted. "If you say so."

She shook her head. Sighed.

At least Marco was being honest. He wasn't promising her something he couldn't give her.

For that reason alone she respected him. Loved him even more, which made the pain of leaving him all the more intense.

But one-sided love was worse than an arranged marriage. She'd seen it in her parents but she hadn't understood how a woman could accept such a situation until she'd experienced it firsthand with Marco.

But, unlike her mother, she wouldn't settle for less than all his heart.

Her time with Marco was over. Now she would begin the process of filing those special memories of them away so she could pull them out and cherish them when her thoughts were clearer, when her heart wasn't aching so much.

"I trust you'll have my paperwork ready for me today." She walked to the doorway he filled so completely, expecting him to at least be a gentleman and move.

He didn't budge, but the muscle along his jawline quivered. She had her choice of trying to push past him or stop. She stopped.

"If that is your wish," he said, his upper lip curling with obvious distaste.

Her wish would be for this to be a bad dream. When she awoke it would be to Marco vowing to love her forever. But that wasn't going to happen.

She tried for a professional smile. "It is."

Because she simply couldn't spend another night in his arms. Already her stomach cramped and her nerves felt raw and frayed at the thought of leaving him. At least if she was busy all day, she could rush to the airport tonight and be gone before her heartache truly set in. Before she surrendered to the flood of tears that were sure to come.

"Anything else?" he asked, voice flat. Emotionless. Sounding as empty as she felt inside.

"I need transportation to the villa to ensure all is well with Bella's wardrobe, then back here so I can oversee that events will run smoothly at the church and the castle."

"Fine," he said, pushing away from the doorway and storming back toward his bedroom. "I'll drive you."

She opened her mouth to argue and then promptly snapped it shut. Avoiding him was going to be impossible so why try?

CHAPTER ELEVEN

MARCO remained silent and brooding as he drove her to St. Antonio de Montiforte Cathedral. She half expected him to abandon her while she double-checked the wedding preparations, but he waited for her, likely impatiently.

The tense silence continued to pulse like a frantic heart beating as he ushered her into his flashy sports car and sped down the highway toward Cabriotini villa. It promised to be the longest hour trapped in an auto that she'd ever endured.

Delanie managed the first ten minutes or so by staring out the window, admiring the scenery. After that she was torn between remaining quiet or making an attempt to talk to him. Neither felt right to her, not when they were at such odds after being so close.

Not when the silence screamed inside her head.

One glance at his set jaw and wounded eyes tore at her heart. She swallowed hard and wadded her fingers together to keep from reaching out to him.

A clean break was needed here. That meant no touching. No softening. Yet she couldn't be that cold, that unfeeling. Not when she felt his pain as deeply as her own.

"I never intended to hurt you or be hurt," she said. "Please believe that."

He didn't answer for the longest time, then finally heaved a sigh and then another. "I know," he said, his voice hushed yet catching. "We seem to excel at inflicting pain on each other."

"Yes," she said, her voice cracking, her chest so tight she could barely draw a breath.

He fell silent again, but then there was nothing left to say. Nothing left to do but get through this day without shedding any more emotional blood.

Once at the villa, Delanie was relieved to find Bella a serene, glowing bride-to-be. Her gown fitted perfectly as did those of her attendants. They were a charming gaggle of young women, some seeming thrilled to be part of such grandeur.

There was simply nothing more for her to do here but ensure that the bridal party would arrive on time. Marco was in charge of that, and she sought him out. No surprise, he was outside standing beside his car.

"I trust you'll be on hand to see that the bride and her attendants arrive at the church on time," she said.

"Her chauffeur will deliver her and her friends in a white limousine, and the housekeeper will see that all leave the villa on time." He nodded to his Bugatti. "If you're ready to return to Montiforte, let's go."

Delanie took a fortifying breath and complied. As on the drive up, silence reigned and tension rose like an ice mountain between them as they sped back to Montiforte.

Marco wheeled under the portico at Castello di Montiforte, and a valet rushed to open her door. She managed a smile as she faced Marco. "Thank you for escorting me about today."

"My pleasure," he said. "The day isn't over. I'll wait for you."

A fact she was all too aware of. "Don't bother. I'm sure you have things to do and I look forward to the walk back."

His eyes narrowed, but their intensity burned stronger. Hotter. "As you wish."

She managed a smile and quickly exited his car, but her legs shook so badly she feared they would give out as she hurried inside the castle. Once there she was able to take a breath, to steer her thoughts on what she must do. That pulled her out of her emotional tumble and allowed her to focus on her job, on doing what she did best.

All the preparations were going well or were finished. All her plans had fallen neatly in order. Her only task was to oversee that nothing unforeseen cropped up to cause a problem.

She refused to think of one sexy Italian as a problem now. Her personal life and her profession could not collide and crash now, not when so much was at stake.

Delanie bit her lip and discreetly checked her watch. In a little over an hour the wedding would commence, followed by the reception. Her hours left in Italy were few. This time tomorrow she'd be back in London.

Her company and her life would be hers to command again. She'd be free of a man's control. Independence would finally be hers.

It was what she'd always wanted, yet there was no excitement in her victory. No reason to gloat.

Not that she could with her heart in tatters.

Love. If she were a cynic like Marco she would swear off ever allowing that emotion into her scope again. But she'd tried to do that with him. And she'd failed.

She downed her head and started up the trail toward the villa. But no matter how many times she mentally went over her checklist, Marco remained the last person commanding her thoughts.

Every second she'd spent with him tormented her. Dammit, she shouldn't be plagued with indecisions now.

They'd struck a bargain. Stuck to it. If she was the weak link and let her heart get involved, that was her problem.

She was making the right choice in leaving. So why did it feel so wrong?

By the time Delanie reached the villa she trembled with nerves scraped raw. Her gaze lit on the Bugatti.

Her body quivered with need and worry, but she tempered

her fears and faced her demons full-on. She stepped into the villa, her gaze searching for him.

Marco stood in the salon, wearing a pale gray suit specially tailored for those broad shoulders that she'd caressed and clung to, the trousers conforming to lean hips that had moved so sensuously with hers. His shirt was black, the bride's choice and befitting the rebel in him.

And she adored the look. Her foolish heart rejoiced at the sight of him. A lonely ache wrapped ghostly arms around her, their touch imagined but not felt.

She shivered, feeling nothing. Knowing that her memories of him were tucked away. If one moment of fabulous sex was enough then she would be blissfully happy. But it wasn't.

It never had been. It never would be, which was why she had to put distance between them now.

"A moment, please," he said as she started to walk past him.

It was a demand, not a question. But then that shouldn't surprise her.

She pushed out a tight breath and stopped, knees locked and toes curling in her sensible flats. "Is something wrong?"

"No."

He crossed to the window, presenting a stiff back to her as he stared through it. She worried her hands together, dreading to know what he wanted to tell her less than an hour before they were to leave for the wedding.

"Is Bella all right?" she asked, worrying that something was wrong, that she might have failed.

He flipped a hand, the motion abrupt. "Bella just called me en route to the church. She is stressed and nervous but otherwise fine."

"Good," she said, hand to her heart. "I was afraid you had bad news."

He faced her then. Grim-faced, solemn and giving her no reason to think that still wasn't the case. Her nerves twitched as he pulled an envelope from his breast pocket and held it out to her.

"You've done everything you said you would do to ensure Bella had the wedding she wanted." His gaze stroked her length once, twice, so personal, so intimate she shivered as if his fingers and hands and tongue had stroked over her willing flesh. "More, actually. There is no reason for me to forestall honoring my promise to you."

By sheer determination, she willed her hand not to tremble as she took the envelope from him, careful not to touch the long blunt fingers that had played over her skin. She slid a nail under the seal and pulled out the papers.

Her mind went numb as she stared at the check and the obscene number of zeros. He'd promised a fat check for professional services.

But this— This was a fortune, far more than she would ever charge a client. Far more than her struggling company was worth.

It was an insult. Wasn't it? A payoff?

Then her gaze landed on the very legal contract. She skimmed it once, heart racing as its significance sunk in.

Elite Affair was hers. All shares reverted to her name only. Her baby. All hers again.

"Why did you do this?" she asked, waving the check, certain the combined value of it and the whole of the company trumped any amount he would give a mistress he'd just dismissed. "What's the catch?"

"There is none."

She sucked in a breath, then another, her mind spinning. "That's hard to believe. Father taught me nothing was free. Nothing good came without a price."

"And I told you to never compare me or the way I work to your father."

"Trust," she said. "We never had that."

"The best lesson my father taught me was never to trust a woman," he said.

"Experience taught me never to trust a man you loved, whether he was a relative or a lover."

His mouth pulled into a flat line and his eyes narrowed to slits, yet enough anger shot from them to make her take a cautious step back. "Point taken. Again. But this is given freely because you deserve a bonus."

"Oh? Then I overreacted," she said and meant it, knowing she'd crossed the line, that she'd insulted him without cause. "I'm just—" How to say it? "Flabbergasted you would do this."

He gave a quick hike of one broad shoulder. "It was wrong of me to hold this over you when it is clear to me now that you were ignorant of your father's plan to destroy me."

She stared at the papers and shivered, far colder inside than she'd been at her father's funeral. But then, this parting was a far different type of grief.

Her father's death had brought relief. Closure.

This parting brought sorrow. No matter how good they'd been at one time, no matter how much better they were in bed, it wasn't enough to make him tear down the walls around his heart. And if he couldn't do that, their passion wasn't enough to make her take him as he was.

She deserved more. They both did, but she was the only one who recognized it.

"That isn't our greatest obstacle, is it?"

He shook his head. "No. We want—expect—different things in a relationship."

He couldn't even bring himself to say *marriage*. It wasn't in his immediate future, and love— Well, love was never part of their equation, at least not mutually.

She wanted his heart. He wanted her body.

On the heels of their brief affair, his largesse came off as a perk for services rendered for work above and beyond the contract. All she'd ever expected was her due, but to argue the point now, before the wedding, just wasn't done.

With strength that was fast slipping, she reminded herself she was the professional here. Making a scene would ruin everything and voicing her opinion would cause a scene.

"Yes, you're right," she said, and managed a smile.

He scowled, his nod coming in an abrupt jerk, his steps toward the door stiff. "I must go to the church now. I'll arrange for a driver to be at your disposal for the rest of your stay."

"Thank you," she managed, waiting for a surge of relief to flow over her.

He stopped on the threshold, fingers splayed on the door frame. "It is I who should thank you." He cut her a look then was gone.

She clutched her hands together, feeling empty. Deserted.

The thud of his footsteps across the terrace was a dirge in her head, signaling the end of their time together. Her shoulders bowed. The raw pain lancing across her heart was simply too much to take after days of so much laughter and passion.

She stared down at the papers that would change her life forever, that gave her the chance to do exactly what she had always wanted. Why wasn't she dancing with joy? Why was she so damned miserable?

The powerful engine on the Bugatti broke the silence, its purr cracking the ice that had held her immobile. She blinked, but her eyes still filled with blinding silent tears.

Somehow she stumbled to the chair by the window, her composure deserting her the second she dropped onto the cushion. Scalding tears poured from her eyes and she let them fall.

If he had insulted her she could have clung to her pride and annoyance and gotten through this. But how could she cope with his polite indifference?

She couldn't and she wasn't about to keep trying.

For the first time in years, she let herself cry over the fact that she and Marco simply couldn't make it work. That they were dynamite in bed. That he could give her anything in this world except the one thing she desperately wanted—his love.

So she cried it all out now, well aware her day wasn't over with him. That she still had hours to get through.

When the emotional storm ended, she hurried to her room and changed clothes, slipping into a simple blue sheath a shade darker than a spring sky.

It fitted her well but was modest. Businesslike. The type of thing she always wore while working. So unlike the lovely dresses and gowns crowding the closet, clothes that Marco had ordered. Clothes she'd refused to try on, let alone wear.

She slipped her feet into taupe pumps and gave herself one last critical look in the mirror. A pale woman with sorrowful eyes stared back at her.

Not the look she wanted to present at the wedding, but how could one erase those lines of heartache? And even if she could, who would really care?

Still, a repair of her makeup, including eye drops, hid the redness in her eyes and minimized the puffiness. A dash of peach blush restored color to her too-pale cheeks.

It was good enough. For the most part, she would be dealing with the workers, not the guests. Surely not Marco. She would do all she could to avoid him, and if their paths crossed and she didn't look her best, so be it.

Their business was concluded. Her wisest course was to do her job and get out of Italy as she'd planned.

Without hesitating, she placed the call to the airline securing a one-way ticket to Heathrow tonight. Then she left her room and focused her thoughts on one thing—ensuring that this wedding went off as perfectly as she'd planned it.

"Marco, why do you look so sad on the happiest day of my life?" Bella asked.

Delanie was the easy answer, and the one that would only prompt a multitude of questions.

"Sorry, my mind was on business," he said, forcing a smile which came easier as his gaze lit on his sister. He wasn't in a mood to answer questions, not on the day that he'd just received word from his CEO at Tate Unlimited who'd found David Tate's hidden personal documents from ten years ago.

The news chilled him. Sickened him. To think he'd believed Tate's lies instead of Delanie. Ass. He'd been a total ass for far too long. *No more!*

Bella looked like a princess in her ivory silk gown that shimmered with threads of ice-green and gold. With a hint of makeup and her hair caught up in some sophisticated style, she was absolutely breathtaking.

"Business," she scoffed, and added an indignant lift of her chin.

He could not help but chuckle. "Tending to business is what has given you a livelihood as well as a dream wedding befitting such a beauty."

She beamed. "I *am* beautiful, yes?"

For a girl born in poverty, she'd learned quickly the nuances of perfecting a haughty demeanor. Of being rich.

"Yes," he said. "You will stop hearts."

Bella clapped both hands together. "There is only one heart I wish to stop and then make race. Giamo's."

The groom, the man she'd fallen in love with and into bed with, was a vineyard worker she'd met right after she'd turned twenty.

Marco had moved out of the estate and into his own home in Montiforte, believing his sister was capable of living by herself. An error on his part, perhaps. But Giamo was a good hardworking man and one Marco believed would one day run the family winery.

Now Bella laughed and twirled before him like a child, looking carefree and far from the expectant mother or bride. Her young-heiress persona was belied on the fact that she still giggled, still could be found in the gardener's shed play-

ing with kittens, still looked too damned young to be a wife
or a mother.

"Delanie is wonderful," Bella said, clasping her hands to
her bosom, totally unaware how mention of Delanie made his
own heart stop and stutter. "You paid her well?"

"A fortune." Which wasn't a lie. He owed her that and more
and not just for her work in planning this wedding.

Bella planted her hands at her waist, her expression suddenly fierce. "Don't let her go, Marco. She is perfect for you.
She would make you a wonderful—"

"Don't say it," he warned, cutting her words off.

"But—"

He slashed the air with a hand, hushing her, the playful
mood shuttered. "There is no *but*. Miss Tate has done a fabulous job planning your wedding just as you requested. Now
she wants to return to her job and her life in England."

His sister scowled. "You're making a horrible mistake letting her go."

"No, I'm giving her what she always dreamed of having,"
he said and believed it. He'd hurt her enough.

Bella tossed both hands in the air, sending her veil fluttering around her bare shoulders, before fixing him with a pitying look. "You should give *yourself* what you've dreamed of
having, Marco. Then you and Delanie would both be happy."

Bella flounced out the door without waiting for his reply,
not that he had one acceptable to voice. In fact, his little sister had rendered him speechless with that observation. How
could one so young be so wise?

He pressed the heels of his hands against his burning eyes
and muttered an oath, sick inside over his lack of emotion.

There had been a time when he had believed money could
buy anything. Had believed that once he was rich, he could
make Delanie happy. And then, of late, had believed that he
would only find peace solo.

Now he knew that was a lie.

Delanie didn't want his wealth. She wanted his love and that was the one thing he didn't know if he could give her.

He'd shut off that emotion years ago, swearing he would never suffer a marriage such as his parents had had, that emotional hell that bound them together and made them—and him—miserable.

"Never be so foolish as to love a woman," his father had told Marco after a particularly violent fight between his parents. "Find a woman who satisfies you in bed, for that is all that a man can expect to have from a woman or a wife. *Amore* poisons. It slowly kills."

That same night, his father had stormed out of the house to find his wife. Only, neither of them had come back.

He shook his head, the pain of that memory faded, replaced by the impending loss of Delanie again. She'd been on his mind since he'd left her this morning.

At the church, his gaze honed in on her the moment she arrived, dressed in an elegant dress befitting a CEO. His chest tightened, his pulse raced, his blood running thick and hot.

He wanted her. Would always want her. But would he cross to her? No!

One of the ushers motioned to him. "It's time."

Marco nodded and followed the man to Bella, who stubbornly refused to look at him.

"I would make her life miserable," he whispered to Bella.

She looked at him with eyes that were suddenly sad. "Oh, Marco. What will it take to make you see that she loves you and that you love her?"

The first strains of "The Wedding March" prevented him from answering that question. He presented his arm to his sister.

"Smile, Bella," he said. "This is your moment."

She held his gaze for a moment then smiled. But the full

force of her beauty didn't shine until they started down the aisle and Giamo turned to face them.

He felt the tremble go through Bella and saw the adoration shining in her eyes and in the groom's. It was a look much like the one Delanie had given him not so very long ago. A look he'd dismissed because the power of it terrified him.

Now the thought of losing that forever scared him more. While everyone's attention was on the bride, his searched out and found Delanie.

Dammit, he wanted her as he'd wanted no other woman. She was his equal in bed and out of it.

But love?

He wished he knew what that emotion was. What it felt like to be caught in its grip. Wanted to know if he was even capable of such feeling.

No great change coursed through him. No miraculous sense that love had suddenly bloomed in the desert that was his heart. No epiphany revealed itself to soothe his soul.

He tore his gaze from hers. For the first time in years, Marco Vincienta felt like a failure.

The sun had set hours ago yet the massive chandeliers hanging from the beamed ceiling cast a mellow glow over tables draped in white linen. Celebrants ate and drank and laughed freely while the wedding singer warbled love songs.

Delanie hovered on the fringe of the massive ballroom, pleased that it had been a perfectly beautiful wedding for Bella and Giamo. The reception at the castle was lovely, with the paparazzi kept outside while Carlo Domanti moved through the crowd, capturing this special day for the happy couple.

A select number of pictures would find their way into the media. Delanie had been promised that a few others would be available to her for advertising purposes.

Everything she'd wanted, needed, to relaunch her business

with flare was now hers. Like the bride, she should be celebrating today as the happiest day of her life.

She *should* have been.

It was sheer torture to know she was excluded from Marco's life now. Her choice. Her hell.

Would it always be this way? Would she always be the fool around this arousing Italian?

If only her gaze didn't constantly swing to him. If only her heart didn't seize and her breath catch at the sight of him laughing and mingling with the guests.

Though for the last hour, he'd been absent. She worried her hands and scanned the crowd. How long did it take for a broken heart to mend?

"This could last all night," came a deep rich voice just behind her.

"Marco," she said, whirling, hand over her thundering heart.

She stared at him, suddenly tongue-tied. Unbelievably at a loss for words.

With effort, she rallied her wits and managed a smile, hoping only she knew that her lips trembled. "You startled me."

"My apologies." He cradled a wineglass in each hand and handed her one.

She took the glass, her fingers barely brushing his. A jolt shot into her veins to set her blood on fire.

He raised his glass to her and smiled and her heart did a tumble again. *"Brava!"*

"To the happy couple." She tore her gaze from his intense scrutiny and focused on the wine, on taking a cordial sip without choking up.

A sudden quietness wrapped around her like a ribbon and had her taking a step closer to Marco before she realized it. His gaze darkened, his lips curving just a smidgeon.

"Cara," he breathed, head bending toward hers.

"Evviva gli sposi!" a guest shouted.

Delanie jumped back from Marco as others joined in with applause and shouts. She raised her glass in the traditional toast, but her heart was still thundering.

If the guest hadn't chosen that moment to salute the bride and groom, Marco's lips would have captured hers. Despite her intentions she would have let them. Welcomed them.

She would have melted in his arms.

The music started up with people hurrying onto the dance floor to form a huge circle.

"Marco, please join us," Bella shouted.

He waved to his sister and extended a hand to Delanie. "You will come too."

Delanie shook her head and retreated another step. "No! I have two left feet and would truly prefer watching. Please, go and enjoy this with your family."

For a moment she was certain he would protest. That he would insist on her participation. But she watched thankfully as he shrugged and strode toward his sister, walking away from her as he must.

Delanie sucked in a breath, painfully aware the time had come for her to leave. That the longer she stayed, the more she risked being seduced by Marco again.

Her job here was over.

Nobody would notice if she left. Nobody would miss her.

CHAPTER TWELVE

AFTER the Tarantella, which seemed endless no matter how enjoyable, had ended, Marco went in search of Delanie. He wasted fifteen minutes before he realized she'd left the castle soon after the dancing began.

No doubt she was exhausted after a day spent overseeing a wedding and reception. The tension he'd added fuel to was a burden she hadn't needed either.

But then that type of behavior should be expected from an ass, and he'd done all in his power the last two days presenting that very image to her. No longer.

He wasn't done with her by a long shot and this time she would hear him out.

The second he fulfilled his duty and saw his sister and brother-in-law off in the wee hours of the morning, Marco sped back to his villa. A gentleman would have waited until morning to confront her, but Marco had proven time and again he was not fully of that league.

Without hesitating, he went straight to Delanie's room. He gave one sharp knock on the door then pushed inside, too impatient to wait for her to rouse from sleep and welcome him in.

Or tell him to go to hell, which was what he deserved!

The dim light from the hall stretched into the room and across the bed—the neatly made bed.

"Delanie," he called out, flicking on the light.

A quick scan of the bedroom confirmed what he already knew in his heart. Delanie was gone.

The only trace of the woman who had occupied his thoughts was the new clothes he'd bought for her, still hanging in the closet untouched.

He stood in the middle of the room, fists bunched at his sides, chest heaving. She'd been so anxious to leave Italy and him that she'd done so tonight.

Not that he blamed her for running off. He was the one responsible for that. He'd driven her away.

He sucked in air, hands fisted, chest heaving as he fought the demon inside him. Letting her go was easy. It was what he'd always done.

Going after her took something he didn't know whether he possessed, something that terrified him. But to lose her forever…

In moments he was behind the wheel again, speeding toward the *autostrada*. He wanted her back, but convincing her that she belonged with him wouldn't be easy. Impossible perhaps.

Giving up wasn't an option. Not now. It was all or nothing.

He had to succeed. Had to make her believe him. The fear that had held his emotions prisoner was nothing compared to the fear of losing her forever.

Delanie paced the waiting area, wondering how much longer it would take for the airline to ready the plane for boarding. Flight times here at night were obviously an estimate and a rough one at that, but there was no other recourse available.

So she paced and she fretted and she tried to think of anything but the tall Italian who'd broken her heart again. It would take time to get over the hurt. Forever to forget him.

"*Attenzione.* Boarding will commence in ten minutes," the clerk said in Italian, and then in English.

Finally, she thought, reaching for the bag at her feet.

"Delanie!" rasped that deep Italian voice that sent chills up her spine. That awakened every nerve in her body to the powerful throb of his presence.

She whirled around and stared at Marco bearing down on her, his hair tousled and face ravaged. His stark white shirt was open at the neck, the bow tie long gone. And then she saw the worry in his eyes and her blood ran cold.

"What are you doing here?" she asked. "Has something gone wrong?"

Not the greeting he'd hoped for. "No. But we need to talk."

"About what?" she asked again.

"Us."

She stiffened, her eyes narrowing. "I can't imagine why."

He dashed fingers through his hair. "You need to know this. My CEO at Tate Unlimited found a hidden stash of your father's papers. In it were documents about your mother's peculiar accidents and Tate's dictate to ensure they stayed hidden. The mark of an abuser, as you'd said. As your mother denied."

She flinched and stiffened. "Fine. You now have proof of what I told you long ago."

"Part of me always believed it," he admitted. "But there's more. There was a written note from your mother to your father dated mere days before he acquired my grandparents' vineyard. She told him about my nonna's failing health. Of my concern. Your mother was the one to betray your trust."

"I'd already come to that chilling conclusion, but I'm glad you know that as well, not that it makes any difference. Now if you'll excuse me—" She turned to leave.

He muttered a curse. So much for thinking the truth would free them of their pasts. That she would greet him with open arms. That she would be as glad to see him as he was to be near her again.

His old fears rushed forward with the warning he'd heeded

all of his adult life. Fool! Trust a woman with your heart and you will end up hurt.

But he already was hurting, his heart aching, his blood pounding so hard his head spun. All his life he'd believed his father's words had kept him from making a mistake with countless women. Then he'd blamed Delanie's betrayal—or what he'd believed was her betrayal—when that wasn't the case at all.

What kept him from committing to any woman was his lack of feeling for those women whose names were long forgotten. All but Delanie. She broke through his defenses. Touched him, even though he'd denied it years ago.

Up until an hour ago he'd still denied it.

Never again. He no longer doubted her word. No longer doubted the feelings surging through his blood. No longer could stand to be apart from her.

Now he knew what was in his heart. He only had to convince her that he was telling the truth.

He stepped in front of her, blocking her way. "If you have nothing to say to me, then you will at least grant me the courtesy of listening while I talk."

Why was he doing this, ripping her heart apart more just by being here? "Sorry, I have a plane to catch."

She grabbed her bag and darted around him, starting toward the shrinking boarding line. He let her take all of two steps before he grabbed her arm and turned her around.

"The damned plane can wait."

Her jaw dropped open, then snapped shut. "It won't wait, even for your arrogance. I'm not about to miss this flight and have to wait another two hours."

The anger he'd wielded like a shield cracked, falling away. His frown deepened as he read the tiredness in her eyes.

"You can't go, Delanie. You can't leave me."

Her shoulders slumped, her fingers clutching her bag when what she really wanted to cling to was him. Stupid, but true.

That's how badly she had it for him still. That's why she couldn't miss this plane.

"I won't stay," she said, staring into his eyes that seemed darker. More intense. More pained. "I won't be your lover."

His big hands cupped her upper arms and did that slow glide down and back up, setting her skin on fire and threatening to melt her fast-fading resistance. "But that is just what you are, *cara mia.*"

She shook her head and found the strength to push him away. "Past tense. What we had is over. I can't go through that again. Goodbye."

She whirled and ran to the check-in, fumbling to pull her boarding pass from her bag. Just a few more seconds and she would board the plane. A few more would carry her away from Marco before her composure deserted her.

"I love you, Delanie Tate," he shouted.

An arctic blast couldn't have froze her in place any quicker. All thoughts of continuing out the door onto the tarmac and the waiting plane were over.

"What?" she asked, turning to face him.

"I love you, *cara.*"

She swallowed, pulse trembling wildly. "You can't be serious."

"Oh, but I am." He nudged her chin up and dropped a kiss on her lips, fleetingly, yet she burned for more. "I loved you ten years ago but was too damned afraid of becoming the same obsessed man as my father. I clung to that belief the past two weeks when all I could think of doing was spending every day and night with you for as long as I lived."

Her gaze probed his and he let her in, let her see the naked soul before her. The barest smile trembled on her lips.

"You aren't just saying the words. You really do love me as I love you," she said, wonder in her eyes, in her smile.

"With all my heart and soul," he said, his lips finding hers again for a long lingering kiss that chased away her doubts, that freed the man she'd fallen in love with years ago.

"Marry me," he said when they finally came up for air. "Stay in Italy with me and run your company. Be my wife. Mother to my children. Balm to my soul."

Her lips trembled and tears sprang to her eyes. This was no joke. No ploy.

This was the declaration she'd waited a lifetime to hear.

She dropped her bag and threw her arms around his neck. "Yes. God, yes!"

His arms banded around her, molding her to his length, oblivious of the stragglers watching. He had Delanie in his arms, in his heart, right where she belonged.

He kissed her forehead, her nose, her inviting lips. "I will make you happy, *cara mia*. I'll make your dreams come true."

She smiled and cupped his face, tears of joy swimming in her eyes. "You already have, Marco. You already have."

* * * * *

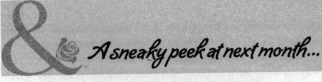

MODERN™

INTERNATIONAL AFFAIRS, SEDUCTION & PASSION GUARANTEED

My wish list for next month's titles...

In stores from 16th November 2012:

❏ A Ring to Secure His Heir — Lynne Graham

❏ Woman in a Sheikh's World — Sarah Morgan

❏ At His Majesty's Request — Maisey Yates

❏ The Ruthless Caleb Wilde — Sandra Marton

In stores from 7th December 2012:

❏ What His Money Can't Hide — Maggie Cox

❏ At Dante's Service — Chantelle Shaw

❏ Breaking the Greek's Rules — Anne McAllister

❏ The Price of Success — Maya Blake

❏ The Man from her Wayward Past — Susan Stephens

Available at WHSmith, Tesco, Asda, Eason, Amazon and Apple

Just can't wait?

MILLS & BOON® Book Club

2 Free Books!

Get your free books now at
www.millsandboon.co.uk/freebookoffer

Or fill in the form below and post it back to us

THE MILLS & BOON® BOOK CLUB™—HERE'S HOW IT WORKS: Accepting your free books places you under no obligation to buy anything. You may keep the books and return the despatch note marked 'Cancel'. If we do not hear from you, about a month later we'll send you 4 brand-new stories from the Modern™ series priced at £3.49* each. There is no extra charge for post and packaging. You may cancel at any time, otherwise we will send you 4 stories a month which you may purchase or return to us—the choice is yours. *Terms and prices subject to change without notice. Offer valid in UK only. Applicants must be 18 or over. Offer expires 31st January 2013. **For full terms and conditions, please go to www.millsandboon.co.uk/freebookoffer**

Mrs/Miss/Ms/Mr (please circle)
_____

First Name
_____

Surname
_____

Address
_____

_____

Postcode
_____

E-mail
_____

Send this completed page to: Mills & Boon Book Club, Free Book Offer, FREEPOST NAT 10298, Richmond, Surrey, TW9 1BR

Find out more at
www.millsandboon.co.uk/freebookoffer

Visit us Online

0712/P2YEA

Special Offers

Every month we put together collections and longer reads written by your favourite authors.

Here are some of next month's highlights— and don't miss our fabulous discount online!

On sale 16th November   On sale 16th November   On sale 7th December